SURVIVAL

7 Nov 1994.

To Vee and Bill
With best wishes
Joan

By the same author
D. I. Y. Tennis

SURVIVAL

Joan Woolley

The Book Guild Ltd
Sussex, England

This book is a work of fiction. The characters and situations in this story are imaginary. No resemblance is intended between these characters and any real persons, either living or dead.

This book is sold subject to the condition that it shall not, by way of trade or otherwise, be lent, re-sold, hired out, photocopied or held in any retrieval system or otherwise circulated without the publisher's prior consent in any form of binding or cover other than that in which this is published and without a similar condition including this condition being imposed on the subsequent purchaser.

The Book Guild Ltd
25 High Street,
Lewes, Sussex

First published 1994
© Joan Woolley 1994

Set in Meridien

Typesetting by Raven Typesetters,
Ellesmere Port, South Wirral

Printed in Great Britain by
Antony Rowe Ltd.
Chippenham, Wiltshire.

A catalogue record for this book is available from the British Library

ISBN 0 86332 952 7

BOOK I

1

Thousands of screams filled the cold February night, ripping the air, as the roof timbers and glass of Liga Station cascaded in balls of flame upon their heads.

'Don't leave me,' shrieked Frau Reinhardt, the leader of the Red Cross group. But everybody did – even Ilse. Too often this hard woman had sneered at her youthful enthusiasm.

Ilse clawed and flailed like a drowning swimmer as she fought with all the instincts of survival to stay upright in the hysterical human tide, swollen with refugees from the east. She mustn't go under. She was dead if she fell beneath those desperate feet. All courtesy was flung aside as people fled before the flames – people who a few moments ago had been sitting patiently on rucksacks, waiting for trains that often never came.

Air-raid sirens and the roar of overhead bombers competed with the anguished cries of those who in great hardship had travelled here in order to be safe. Heat and fumes devoured precious air. Burning debris showered down upon them. The last train had gone. Any loved ones waiting to meet them at the other end of the line would wait and wait.

'Will all passengers please go to the basements,' requested the loudspeakers.

'No. This way,' someone yelled at her as they burst

into the street. All Ilse saw was another wall of flames but she followed the voice. Colossal winds lifted and speeded her. She knew then it was true about the survival of the fittest. Many were not going to make it tonight. It was a young woman with auburn hair who had shouted, Ilse saw now in the glow of the fire-storm. The crowd thinned. Some never reached the street. Shortly after Ilse bludgeoned her way under the arched entrance, it collapsed, sealing in those still in the station.

Choking on the vicious smoke, she sprinted through the burning streets. Mutti, Vati – she must find Mutti and Vati. In panic she followed the woman. The Gothic buildings fell in molten avalanches of masonry. Dark running figures screamed. A frantic horse, still in circus finery, ran with them. It was so hot, they could scarcely breathe. A giant tree rose out of the earth as if it were an oriental house on stilts. Furiously burning branches threw out sparks. The woman was on fire. Ilse, assisted by the biting teeth of the tornado-strength wind, ripped off her own coat. In a despairing tackle she brought her to the ground, pummelling and beating her to douse the flames. Only the thickness of their coats and the width of the street saved them. Wordlessly they got up and ran on.

'We must find a cellar,' someone shouted.

'No,' yelled Ilse's companion. 'The embankment.'

Ilse followed, panic lending strength to her legs. Mutti always said, 'The most powerful human instinct is survival; the next is sex.' She understood. The woman veered to the left and disappeared. Had she fallen? Ilse was terrified.

I can't breathe. Mutti, Vati, I'm dying.

Choking on the hot smoke, she sank to the ground. It felt like the bottom of a volcano. Arms enfolded her, dragging her down into a hole. Someone muttered in a foreign language. There was a swish of liquid as a beer-soaked cloth was clamped over her face. She didn't know what happened next. Perhaps she passed out?

Later that night a head smelling of beer and medicaments murmured, 'I'm Michelle. What's your name?'
'Ilse. My parents? Are they all right?'
'I don't know. Where do they live?' asked the educated voice.
'Spatz Holz.'
'They may be lucky. They seem to be bombing the centre. We couldn't have been in a worse place.' It was hot in the cavern, but air circulated. She looked around her. The earth walls were lined with stoical, unblinking faces.
'Forced labourers from the east. They're laying power lines. They speak hardly any German. Ukrainians, I think,' whispered Michelle.
The planes had gone. After the assault the silence made their ears pop. They peered out of the entrance.
'We're just above the railway line. I live near here. That's how I knew where to run,' said Michelle, her head close to Ilse's, as like animals scenting whether the coast is clear, they wriggled cagily out of their lair.
'Must get home.' Ilse rubbed her watery eyes anxiously.
'What are you going to do?'
'I'll stay put for a while. If I can get through I'll make for Mother's. Look, it's clouding over. If it stays overcast they may not be back.'
'Where can I find you again?' asked Ilse.
'Heinrichgasse 30 or at the station. I'm a GP but I've just started doing nights with the wounded back from

the front.' Worriedly she looked skywards. 'Run like hell, won't you. You never know.' She took some swabs from her bag. Soaking them with beer she fitted them inside a surgical mask. 'Here put this on.'

'I don't know how to thank you.' Ilse took Michelle's hand in both of hers.

'Follow the railway line,' continued Michelle. 'That'll bring you out at the woods above Spatz Holz and . . . good luck.'

'Good luck,' echoed Ilse, easing herself along a ridge.

Before making her way down the steep incline to the track, she lay flat on her stomach, squirming her way up to the bank's summit, and looked back towards the station. Dense smoke swirled around her. The eastern sky was lit as if a thousand bonfires had joined into one. There was the roar of hell. She slid down, grasping at stems of shrubs along the way. Losing her footing, she rolled herself into a ball as she toppled over scrub and earth and pot-holes. Her back jarred as she hit clinker packed around the railway sleepers. For a while she just lay there, the pain insignificant compared with. . . .

Through the smoke and the night she ran and walked and stumbled westwards, overtaking hordes of others fleeing staring-eyed along the same route. She came to a long catacomb of a railway tunnel. Petrified by the dark and the gnawing sounds, she plunged onwards, banking on the certainty that there would be no trains running tonight. It seemed endless, but eventually when almost worn out she saw a pinhead of light. Oh, the relief as she recognized where she was. Up the embankment to the left was the familiar turnip pile which she passed twice weekly on her foraging trips to outlying farms. After reaching this landmark she could almost taste the pines' coolness on her tongue. Half running, sometimes falling, she staggered down the path that led to home.

The gate was open, the house dark. In the deserted kitchen a bread knife and half-cut loaf lay on a board. She hammered on the cellar door, the rough wood reddening her knuckles with blood. The sound of a latch lifting, and she fell through an open doorway. Her parents' malnourished faces marvelled at the sight of her. Neighbours offered potato soup from flasks, then came the sleep of exhaustion.

Below, raged incineration on a grand scale; in a city jammed with children, old people, women civilians, prisoners of war, refugees fleeing the Red Army, military personnel on leave and the wounded who had come home.

2

The quiet of the morning was terrible. The cloud of endings seemed to have passed over the sun. Stiff and aching, Ilse, her parents and the elderly neighbours who were too old for war duty emerged blinking into the half-light. No one spoke as they filed out into the garden. On clear days one could see a long way from this wooded hillside. This morning they saw nothing save a huge ball of sinister yellowy smoke. Small pieces of paper and charred particles wafted across the lawn on the westerly wind. An acrid smell of something indescribable clung stickily to everything. They all knew someone who might not wake in this centre of culture and beauty, its heart gouged out in a few hours.

Ilse took her mother's arm. 'Mutti, can you eat something?'

'No, *Liebling*. Not yet. You get something. You must see if there is work to do.' Frau Weinacht felt so tired. Two world wars in her lifetime, her parents' bankruptcy when she was in her teens, leaving Czechoslovakia, the country of her birth, when she married Wilhelm, her husband repeatedly passed over for promotion because he did not join the Party, and now this. She thanked God for bringing Ilse safely home. How long before the Russians came? All these thoughts she would not share with her husband and daughter. These days many things were never put into words. The dread was too enormous. You tried not to think about it.

Ilse left the silent group and went up the flagstone steps by the side of the house. The bird who usually sang in the climbing creeper was absent. She put together some slices of butterless bread, added half a black sausage and, together with a flask of water mixed with flour and residue from potato peelings, placed them in her rucksack and set off for work.

Where the tree-line met suburbia there was nothing. Numbly she looked at the carnage. Once-opulent houses with balustraded balconies — many of which had been split into flats — were gone. So were the lush gardens overhung with trees, some over two hundred years old. It was as if some malignant giant had swished a massive scraper over the land. Now they were piles of smoking rubble from which there would be a sudden lick of flame as if a wild animal was guarding its kill. Other buildings still burned.

Outer, her first boyfriend, the one who had gone to sea as a submarine officer, had lived here. His mother? Where was she? Safe in the cellars? The atmosphere was horrible. Not a blade of grass anywhere; just molten heavings of broken concrete peppered with cobbles. She started to scrabble amongst the stones, then lunged back as if shot. The rubble just beneath the surface covering glowed red-hot.

'Frau Zeiler, Frau Zeiler,' she screamed.

Silence. A disgusting smell of singed rubber rose. Her shoes were smoking. She lifted one of her feet to look underneath. A hole had burned right through sole and sock. The ground was too hot to walk on. From her rucksack she took some small towels. Mutti had cut up a large bath towel, converting it to several hand-towels and babies' nappies. She carried these with her in case of an opportunity to exchange them for food. Rocketing inflation made bartering a necessity. Every morning you looked for things that could be swopped so that you might eat that day. Ilse bound her feet, hoping the reinforced footwear would last long enough to get her to the Red Cross post.

Nearby was the site where the tram terminus had been. It had been swept away. The shop from which Greta dispensed coffee and smiles was no longer. After a particularly heavy or upsetting shift and when the weather was good, Ilse would sit on one of the chairs outside. It was pleasant to unwind before the trek up the hill to home. As the mellow sunshine seeped through her weary body she would sip coffee and swop a newly-discovered joke with Greta, never tiring of the haunting beauty of the Jugendstil houses opposite.

Over there was more debris and something about a metre high. It had been red-hot. Now it was moulded into a rigid sculpture. There was one large object and another smaller one. She looked closely, not yet wise enough not to scrutinize anything too much if she wanted to retain her sanity. Leaping back in horror she felt the sick rising. A human hand. A large one welded to a smaller one. The other bound to the twisted frame of a pushchair. There was no face; just the pose of a form bent protectively towards the ground.

The heat burned through the towels. The fire-storm had tortured the buildings in such a way that they spread over large areas, making the roads impassable. Ilse ran for home as fast as the uneven and smoking ground would allow. Tears blinded her. Why that child and not her? The infant had no chance now to know the walks in the romantic woods, the dancing class, the Sunday walks all dressed in white, tea and picnics with friends. She felt no answer to her question.

3

Though desperate to help, it was next day before the heat abated sufficiently for Ilse to penetrate the city centre. All communication systems had broken down, yet she joined columns of helpers marching towards the eye of the receded storm.

Huge convoys of trucks laden with rescue gear and soldiers, civilians with handcarts, Red Cross vehicles loaded with food, baby requirements and medical supplies collected at the city outskirts. So many and yet not a sound. Hands, yearning to be useful, reached out to carry something. They must make their payment for being alive. The horizon, the like of which they had never seen before, and documents and shop contents bearing inner city addresses and labels blown into their gardens on the virulent winds, told them more than any radio or telephone could.

Ilse joined an over-young contingent from the League of German Girls unit. Together they loaded themselves with as much as they could carry and joined the rhythm of tramping feet of this self-appointed army. All roads to the central square looked impenetrable but like a legion of invading ants they would not be stopped. Soldiers wielding inadequate shovels and picks set to work.

'*Gott steh' uns bei!*' said one, 'God help us. Must've been some fire,' as he looked incredulously at the melted bricks. Not a complete building was to be seen. For as far as the eye could see, the ashscape was broken only by half-walls of ground floors of apartment blocks that once had risen five and six storeys high. Now they looked like upended coffins.

Even though the Russians had been advancing since the autumn, city life continued as before. Theatre-goers had been ambling home. Bars disgorging satisfied customers. Soldiers going home to their families. Street-dwellers seeking suitable shelter. The young of the town beginning their night shift, aiding refugees seeking food and temporary lodging. Just another wartime night.

As the sirens gathered volume, people like Ilse and Michelle had abandoned their posts and run for their lives. Escape from the flames meant open spaces, river and railway banks. Countless numbers had not made it. Now they lay stripped of clothes, their faces still wearing an expression of torment at what they had seen. Others looked as though they had simply fallen asleep. Still more had shrivelled into bizarre shapes and melted with the tarmac as it boiled. Ilse was walking on bodies. The unlucky, the old, the disabled, the ones whom the merciless wind had gathered in its paths.

The heat had transformed vast tracts of city into billions of particles which had moved upwards, hiding the sun, if indeed it shone today. It was a beleaguered place that received the rescue workers and food-bearers with scarcely a response – there were too few of the living. Around the largest rubble heap of all stood a group of dark-coated people, their faces seemingly etched into a background of ash. There came sounds of dragging as large bundles of what appeared to be old clothes were piled outside the station door.

'Oh, aren't we lucky? Miss Goody-Goody has finally

condescended to join us,' cackled a hysterical voice nearby.

'Oh, Frau Reinhardt, it's you. I'm sorry. There were no trams.'

'No trams – no trams – no trams – she says there are no trams.' Dancing wildly, Frau Reinhardt, with an arm at a grotesque angle and her hair uncombed and flying, made a peculiar sight.

Michelle's head popped out of the flap door of a crude tarpaulin shelter hastily erected by the Party Welfare Organization.

'She's flipped. I need help. Get the clothes off this one.' Michelle attended to the next whilst Ilse obeyed instructions. The burned skin and garments were melded. Was it a man or a woman?

'Too late,' said Ilse.

Michelle shouted. Two men took it away.

'I'm running out.' Momentarily Michelle closed her eyes. When she opened them no miracle had happened. The stock of ointments and pain-killers was going down fast.

'Don't worry. The Red Cross vans are coming. I passed them.' Ilse noticed how white and tired Michelle's face was. The heightened adrenalin flow of escape was gone. But her hair was still a glorious auburn in the daylight.

Michelle wiped her hand down a filthy raincoat. 'The water's no use. The sewer pipes have burst. We can't risk it. This lot need a hospital.'

'One of the drivers said they're using more schools down river as hospitals. The pupils are manning the boats and they're on their way,' offered Ilse.

'God, I've never felt so helpless in my life,' ranted Michelle in a furious whisper so only Ilse could hear. 'Your parents? Are they OK?'

'Yes. Your mother?'

'I haven't been home yet.' Michelle's lips almost disappeared as her mouth set in a thin line.

'Doctor Weidel,' shouted one of the rescue workers, and a heavily lined face poked through the slit in the tent. Dieter was on permanent staff at the station and head of the group of technical workers. He had been directing the digging.

Treading carefully, Michelle accompanied him to the recently opened hole which led to the basement vaults. Before entering they shouted, 'Hello. Can you hear us? We're coming to help.'

They tried again. There was nothing. Dieter inched his way through the opening. He was gone for quite a while. No sounds came out of the darkness. Then suddenly, amid clothes tearing and elbows grazing, he shot out of the hole as though he had seen something terrible. His mouth worked incoherently as he stood with his arms clutching and unclutching feverishly across his chest. Then he covered his face with his hands. Through split and bleeding fingers, in his fast, guttural dialect he managed the words, 'They're all in there. Thousands of 'em. Just sleeping. All leaning up against each other, just sleeping.'

Rescue work in other areas stopped. Embattled, malnourished, with weary legs buckling, they drifted over to the spot on which had stood one of the busiest main-line stations in Europe, whose platform had felt the tramp of millions of migrating feet. A dividing line between those alive and the dead hardly existed. The living had seen more than they could cope with. At least the dead were spared the struggle for survival.

In the vault was somebody's child, somebody's parent, somebody's lover.

4

A stubbly group of Fire Protection Police trudged into the clearing. They reported for duty at the temporary Party HQ. From the back of a horse-drawn wagon that had rumbled along the only track into the inner city, they were issued with digging equipment, gas masks, rubber boots – rubber gloves were unavailable, the stock having perished in the fire – and strong drink with which to overcome the stench of decay that pervaded as bodies rotted.

Michelle and Ilse took Dieter to the mobile kitchen. The black coffee sploshed onto the ground as his hand shook. The chief of the fire police joined them. He and Michelle had met before, during other air raids in the area.

'What sort of time have you had?' asked Michelle, looking pointedly at the burned wreckage of his sleeve.

Herr Grense spread his hands to the heavens and in a smoke-affected voice said, 'There was nothing we could do. We've teams stationed in the outlying villages but they couldn't get through. We still haven't heard what's happened to them. We got the people out of the theatre, but only a few made the canal and those who couldn't swim dragged down those who could.' He rubbed his unshaven chin and looked down at the ground, kicking with his foot a half-buried leg iron. Michelle's caring face looked at him in sympathy.

A horse, its ornate bridle hanging loose and sometimes tripping him, entered the square. Ilse recognized the scarlet and gold saddle. It was the circus horse that had run with them down the road from the station on the night of the attack. Now it was lame and piteously whimpering, its hooves and once beautiful Arabian legs were smeared with tar. Wounds gaped from dapple-grey flanks. Deeply distressed, it swayed and nearly fell over. Herr Grense put down his coffee cup and sought to calm the animal. His team-mates joined him, and they soothed its trembling. Michelle filled a syringe and ended its misery. The horse – a symbol of joy and fun – sank to the ground sighing; then it rolled over and was gone from them.

'My baby, my baby,' wailed a prowling Frau Reinhardt.

'I didn't know she had a baby,' said Ilse.

'Her son died in the First World War,' Michelle explained. 'She told me once when she was drunk. Perhaps it explains a lot of things.'

'I didn't know you knew her.'

'I usually went to the station at nights. That's when the casualties came in. She was sometimes on duty.'

'How on earth did we miss each other – I occasionally do nights.' Ilse looked again at Frau Reinhardt, who was now sitting down hugging herself. 'We've all got our problems.'

Handcart after loaded handcart started arriving.

'It's a transport problem now. These people need a hospital.' Michelle went to confer with a medical team from the next town. She returned to Ilse, saying in a voice like a child who wants to go home, 'I must see Mum.' But she suddenly looked older than her late twenties.

'I'll come with you. It's pretty gruesome out there on your own,' said Ilse.

'Oh, would you? You'll like Mum.'

'If she's anything like you,' smiled Ilse, 'I've no doubt. What'll we do about *her*?' And she pointed to their wandering head nurse.

'Oh hell, I suppose she'll have to come along. She's got nobody, as far as I can gather.'

They rounded up the older woman.

'Come on, love,' said Michelle, taking her good arm. Ilse followed behind.

5

No drop of water ever felt so good as the first that splashed onto Ilse's upturned face. The squall that followed was beautiful – a real gift from heaven. They opened their mouths and held their hands out, drinking in the purity; so different from the unfriendly liquid that bubbled from thousands of water-pipe fractures. Even the madwoman was a relief, her incoherent patter and songs diverting attention from the unlookable at as they slowly threaded their way home. Occasionally a horribly scorched face would poke out of a hole in a ruin, then pop back like a rabbit down a burrow. Curling up in a dungeon was a lesser evil than the street.

Since leaving the station, Michelle had been quiet. Now she broke out into highly strung chatter.

'We had to leave our farm when Dad died. Onkel Felix was Dad's brother – that's how we came to Liga. He ran a restaurant in Wirtsgasse. He needed help and we had no home. Then they took him away. We've never heard from him since. When we made enquiries we were told he had committed a traffic offence. The restaurant folded – not enough supplies. The bit Dad left paid for my medical training and I was eventually able to support Mum.'

Overhead, mangled wires and cables writhed and fought like serpents. A tram, its contents macabre, lay on its side, squashed and buckled to a third of its size. An elderly woman dressed in black hurried by. Her eyes had a desperate stare.

'Don't look,' she whispered to the little one by her side. Protectively she turned the child's face into her skirts.

'Bergermeisterstrasse. We're here,' said Michelle, biting her lip. Frau Reinhardt had piped down.

'They're all five storeys along here – were. Private landlords. We were lucky with ours. Herr Bergermeister was a friend, and his son took over. They're in coffee. The rent's very reasonable. No cellar though. I expect Mum's with her friend across the road. That side have large cellars.' Michelle spoke rapidly as if speech might keep the truth away. Frau Reinhardt hummed. Ilse was mute. She couldn't think of a single thing to say that would comfort.

'There's Hans – you know, the one I was telling you about. Runs the coffee warehouse in the next street.'

She ran up to him. Two metres of reassurance and greying ginger smiled with pleasure at the sight of Michelle. It struck Ilse that it was the first smile she had seen since before their flight.

'Hans, thank God. You're all right?' She kissed his whiskery cheek, then turned to look at her home. Desecration. He looked away. She put off asking the question.

'Hans, this is Ilse. We escaped from the station that night. She saved me in the streets.'

Ilse shook her head vehemently. 'No, she saved me.'

Hans bowed his head and shook hands with her. Michelle turned to where Fran Reinhardt was plucking at the burn marked sleeve of her injured arm.

'And this is Frau Reinhardt, head nurse at the station.'

'Have you seen my baby?' Frau Reinhardt asked Hans.

Looking at the distraught woman, Hans discreetly summed up the situation.

'I'm afraid I haven't, ma'am,' he said, and kissed her hand.

'See, a real gentleman. Some people treat me proper,' she squeaked, looking defiantly at Ilse.

The deep brown of Michelle's eyes glistened as they asked Hans for the answer she did not want to know. As if lifting a baby from a cradle, he placed his huge hands round her shoulders.

'We can't be certain yet.' He didn't patronize her. 'Tomorrow it will be cool enough. Plenty have been perfectly OK.'

Michelle broke from his gentle touch. Screaming hysterically, she scrabbled at the rubble. 'Mummy, Mummy.' She flung stones around in a frenzy. The others backed off. She reached the masony beneath the surface.

Seeing the danger, Ilse shouted, 'No,' and grabbed her friend's hands. As she did so, layers of mutilated skin stuck to hers. She buried Michelle's head into her shoulder, comforting her.

'We're coming back tomorrow. As Hans says, most of the cellars are in good shape. They'll be all right.' She stroked the sobbing head whilst looking despairingly at Hans.

'Thank you,' she mouthed, 'I'll take her home.'

'Where can I find you?' he asked. She gave him her address, then with an arm round Michelle and a hand holding Frau Reinhardt's, they stumbled down the unrecognizable street littered with cars and people whom death had frozen in flight.

They had not gone far before Michelle broke from them.

'My case,' she gasped, running over to where it lay, its battered corners now no longer frayed but singed and alive from the hot bricks Michelle had unearthed. She banged out the smoulder and snapped open the bag. Using a sheet torn from her prescription pad and a length of sticking plaster, she attached a note for her mother to the stub of a lamp-post. Ilse stretched out her hand. Michelle took hold. When they looked back, Hans was standing with sunken head, staring at the ground, his hands deep in his coat pockets. The note fluttered lonesomely as though waving goodbye.

The three of them sat down. They had reached the forest area. From here there was a steep climb to the houses perched at the end of a multitude of criss-crossing cart-tracks. Ilse's father had inherited their house from his father, an antique dealer and art historian. Their eyes drank greedily of the greenery. It looked like paradise.

'Grass,' sighed Michelle and lay down, burying her face in the naturalness. 'Mum and I often talked about going back to the country when the war is over.' Michelle's knuckles clenched white as she clasped and unclasped hands that hugged her knees to her chest.

'Oh *shut* up,' shouted Ilse to Frau Reinhardt, who was beginning another of her songs. She slapped the woman on the cheek.

Frau Reinhardt held her face, saying ominously, 'Young lady, you'll come to a sticky end, you will.'

Ilse looked in horror at her hand and then at Michelle, whose face was buried in her arms as she sat foetus-like on the bank. 'I've never done anything like that before.'

Without looking up, Michelle replied, 'We'll probably do a lot of things we've never done before.' She unfurled herself and got up.

Bent and in single file, they climbed the path to home.

6

The white stucco house with balconies and verandah-encircled ground floor welcomed them. Though February, the back door was flung wide. With the rains had come a mild spell that brought respite to the homeless.

'Mutti, Vati,' shouted Ilse, knowing well how lucky she was to be able to use those words. A woman nearing fifty appeared in the doorway, quietly dressed in a dark pinstripe skirt suit, a full-collared white blouse showing against the jacket's wide lapels. Her dark hair was drawn back to a small coil at the nape of the neck, a sprinkle of grey showing to the right of her widow's peak. Perfectly positioned blue-grey eyes under dark eyebrows arched like birds' wings appraised the situation, and the three worry lines between her eyes and the creases that ran from nose to mouth corners seemed to deepen as she saw more fully their distress.

'Come in please, all of you.' The serene voice acted like ointment on their wounds. Just to shed responsibility for a short time was heaven.

'Mutti, this is Michelle – you know, the one who helped me escape – and this is Frau Reinhardt, who is in charge of our Red Cross post. She's ill and has nowhere to go.'

Frau Reinhardt squatted down on the wooden slatted floor of the verandah, dangling her legs over the edge and humming as her blank eyes looked in the direction of the sloping garden. Michelle saw the question in Frau Weinacht's eyes as she noticed the limp arm.

'Don't worry, I'll fix a splint.'

Mutti bent down and touched Frau Reinhardt's shoulder. 'Come inside, my dear.'

As always, the kitchen was dark. The power lines had been destroyed, so there was no electricity. Even before the raids each household had been on a strict ration of watts, and was fined if it exceeded this limit. Their next-door neighbours had left a light on all week and were forced to sit in darkness all the following week in order to recoup the wasted power.

Ilse's father and his brother's widow, Frieda Weinacht, sat on a bench alongside the scrubbed table. Vati's dome-shaped head was almost bald, and behind his small gold-coloured rimmed spectacles his eyes twinkled like Ilse's, although the humour lines were deeper. He stretched his arms out to his daughter.

Ilse went to him. She kissed his forehead. 'To think. . . .' She did not finish the sentence as she cuddled him.

As Michelle watched, she silently continued the sentence for Ilse. The vagaries of the station shift system and luck were all that had stood between this family group and. . .

Herr Weinacht stood up and shook Michelle's offered hand. 'I've seen you at the station. You work very hard.'

'Thank you,' said Michelle, smiling. 'And thank you for taking us in.'

'It's our pleasure, although I must apologize. We haven't much to offer you, I'm afraid. No light, no hot water; but we do have food. We're lucky, I'm able to get extra rations if I work overtime.'

Frau Reinhardt looked agitated. Her mouth began to open. Ilse, who was sure it would be something inappropriate, hushed her.

'We'll take you up for a bath in a minute.'

Frieda Weinacht, a healthy colour from manning the garden turned vegetable plot, her face a patchwork of tiny square wrinkles, turned to Michelle.

'You look worn out.' Then she gasped, 'Your hands! Ursula, get the first aid. We'll warm some coffee. My brother-in-law has a friend at work who is able to get us paraffin.' Sparrow-like she darted from her seat to the glory-hole under the stairs and dragged out a small paraffin stove. 'It's been a godsend.'

Michelle smiled wearily, admiring this middle-class family's pride in their wheeler-dealing. She was so glad to let someone else do the organizing and thinking. She had nothing more to give today. Seated next to Vati, she leaned against the wall, closing her eyes for a while as Ilse took Frau Reinhardt upstairs to clean her up.

'Call when you're ready. I'll fix that arm,' Michelle shouted after her.

Mutti heated water on the stove, carefully measuring out some flour, then chopping the meagre two ounces of fish that would have to do for six people. She and her sister-in-law were on death card rations, which amounted to barely one thousand five hundred calories per day. They were classed as housewives, a different category from those who were employed, and yet the energy they put into walking many kilometres to queue for hours and working on their garden plot to eke out their vegetable supply left them permanently tired. Vati and Ilse got more rations because they were in employment. When they worked extra time, the household ate just above starvation level.

There was a knock at the door. The occupants of the

kitchen froze. There were question marks in Mutti's eyes as she looked at Vati. He shook his head in a 'don't know' way. Michelle went white, staring hard at her roasted hands. Tante Frieda carefully laid aside her knitting and quickly slipped the paraffin stove back into its hiding-place, then bent-shouldered, legs working fast, she disappeared down the hallway to answer the door.

A young man in despatch rider's uniform stood on the step.

'A note for Herr Weinacht, ma'am,' he said.

'Wilhelm, for you,' shouted his sister-in-law.

Herr Weinacht moved quickly despite his bulk.

'Thank you,' he said, taking the note. He did not invite the lad in for refreshment. No one knew who was carrying information to whom, and no spare food was to be had anywhere.

Tensely Mutti asked, 'What is it, Wilhelm?'

'They want me in at first light tomorrow. It's urgent they open a line. I don't know where I'm going to find the men.' Herr Weinacht was a director of engineers. Despite his bosses finding him politically uncooperative, he was tolerated, his expertise being vital to the running of the transport system.

In the last saucepan they owned – one had been lent to a neighbour in return for a favour and the rest had been bartered – Mutti warmed the evening meal.

'At least we'll all be together tonight. Ilse'll have to go to the country tomorrow.' She and Ilse would rummage yet again for things to exchange. Her daughter was turning food-foraging into an art form. She rarely came back empty-handed and had developed a network of contacts which she revealed to no one. Sometimes she went north through the woods and was gone for most of the day. Other times, together with hundreds of food-seekers, she hung onto the outside handles of railway carriages, to get a lift to new areas.

Ilse came downstairs with a subdued, well-scrubbed Frau Reinhardt, who looked rather snug in a pink quilted housecoat. It was one of Mutti's conversions from a bedspread. They had been going to sell it, but now it would have to go on loan to their house guest. Frau Reinhardt's clothes were too far gone. Still, they could salvage something from them to go towards making something else. Nothing, but nothing, must be wasted.

Vati pulled out a chair for their guest. 'May I know your first name, Frau Reinhardt?' he asked politely.

'Katja,' she whispered, as though it was a long time since anyone had called her that name.

'I don't know how you do it, Ursula,' he smiled at his wife. 'The things you manage to cobble together on that old sewing machine.'

Katja stretched out her good arm in order to get a better look at the new garment. She fingered it disbelievingly. Vati finished laying the table with spoons. Knives and forks would not be needed as there was no butter or meat today.

'Did I hear you say you would be going into work tomorrow, Herr Weinacht?' asked Michelle.

'That's right. Very early though.'

'May I walk with you? I must find out about. . . .' Her voice petered out as if she couldn't say the word.

'We'll sort everything out. You come with me,' said Vati, anxiously glancing at Ilse, who had joined them at the table.

'I'm sure they'll need me at the station, especially nights,' added Michelle. There was silence. She and Herr Weinacht knew what came in at night.

Safe for a while from bombers and Russians, the six

adults shared their meal of water, flour, fish and dried bread. Michelle ate quickly. This was her first food since the cup of coffee with Dieter at the *Hilfszug*, the mobile kitchen. Hardly believing in this feeling of safety she looked around the table. There was a light in Ilse's eyes that drew her. As though centuries peeled away. As though they had always known each other.

7

It was still early in the year, and darkness closed in before afternoon had ended. Uneasy twilights. A sunless, mole-like existence dominated by the deprivation of necessities. Silesian winds knifed through skeletal bodies, rattling the black-out blinds. Getting food was all. Rats gnawed. Wolves moved nearer town, joining with the humans in the national scavenge. In her makeshift bedding comprising brown wrapping paper from far off Christmases, precious old newspapers and a nearly bald fur coat, Ilse would shudder at their howling. Memories. Sunlit vignettes. Dances. Linking arms with handsome young men. Flirting. Walking in the woods. Stopping for real coffee and *torte* at the Country Club. Where were their ambitious know-it-all companions now? Dead? Dying for what? Their girls back home – the ones who used to wear pretty check dirndl skirts were dying also, only they did it more slowly.

'Drink this, Katja.' Mutti gently guided the rocking woman to the kitchen table. 'It's a concoction from our herb garden. My sister-in-law's rather good on that sort of thing. Family secrets.' Mutti glanced affectionately at the furiously knitting Tante Frieda.

'All kinds of homoeopathic wonders come out of their black cauldron. Mutti and Tante Frieda are well-known locally. They come from far and wide for their potions. Just don't ever ask what's in them. It'd make you ill,' giggled Ilse.

'Now now,' said Mutti, shaking a finger at her daughter. Katja allowed the liquid to be table-spooned down her throat.

'Ilse, get some beds organized. Take a blanket from our bed and one from Frieda's. There are newspapers under the stairs. Katja'll go in with Frieda and Michelle with you.'

Ilse turned to Michelle. 'Are you ready for turning in yet?'

Exhaustedly Michelle nodded. She turned in the doorway. 'I don't know how to thank you.'

They were not a family of unnecessary words. They simply looked at her as a family would.

'I'll leave a flask here.' Mutti pointed to the draining board.

'Half past seven?' asked Vati.

'Thank you. Good night.'

The knitting needles clicked and Katja hummed a mournful tune.

Before climbing the stairs the two young women collected the oddments along the way that would go towards creating the makeshift bedding.

'Help me with this,' said a voice from beyond the rear end sticking out of the glory-hole. Ilse dragged an antiquated camp-bed from its roost amongst the spiders. The rents in the canvas had been patched with a multitude of coloured pieces of material but it still looked hell-bent on distintegration. They humped the thing upstairs and into Ilse's back bedroom.

'Wall-to-wall fitted linoleum.' Ilse puffed her chest out proudly. 'Carpets bartered like everything else. Vati discovered a talent for making rugs from them. One farmer had killed a pig and acquired a new wife. We needed the pig. He needed the rugs for the marital boudoir. Supply and demand. Supply and demand.'

For the first time Michelle couldn't help but relax. She grinned at the irrepressible Ilse.

'Ilse the wheeler-dealer. After the war it's got to be the antique trade for you.'

During the night the rain lashed. The usual wolf sounded closer than normal. Ilse told herself she would never again take a roof over her head for granted. She tossed restlessly in the second-hand bed, bought when her parents were starting out on family life. It was solid oak and so high off the ground she almost needed a step-ladder to get in. A butterfly was carved on the bed head.

Below her lay Michelle on the camp-bed, wrapped around in Vati's railway-issue greatcoat. She saw her friend shiver. There was a gap between sill and blackout blind. The light allowed her to see the two rivulets of tears running down Michelle's face. Ilse stretched out a hand to touch her shoulder.

'Michelle, you're freezing. Come in with me. Let's put the coats together.' The dry paper crackled. Fully clothed, they huddled together, creating a warmth in the bleakness of the unheated bedroom. As if to smooth away the anguish lines that threatened to become permanent, Ilse's rough working hand lightly rested on her friend's forehead. Michelle slept – Ilse hardly at all.

8

It was still dark when Ilse woke. The concave space next to her was cold. Michelle had been gone some time. Oh God, what news would she bring home tonight? Would she come back?

Ilse decided she would have to go sick from work today. Not a difficult thing to do. The world they knew had gone and Katja Reinhardt was in no position to issue punishment.

Mutti and Tante Frieda did the local queuing. Ilse did the long-distance stuff. The advantage of employment was the increase in ration allowance and the opportunity for overtime. The down side was the reduction in exchange and bargaining time.

Reluctantly removing the layers of antiquated pullovers, she had a perfunctory wash in the cold water in the basin on the dressing-table. Running water now came under Grade A luxury item. Every day Mutti walked down the hill to the stand-pipe; filled as many containers as she could carry; then walked back up. Conditions were not far removed from those of the African woman at the well, her water pitcher balanced upon her head. Every drop was liquid gold.

She dreamed of those breakfasts of long ago as she sat stiffly down on the seat by the walnut kidney-shaped dressing-table. She felt like a skeleton moving beneath a skin bag. Surely her stomach would collapse. The meagre contents might as well not be there for all the good they made her feel. Elbows supported by the table top, she briefly rested her head in her hands and then did the necessary preparations. From the top drawer she pulled out a grease-stained check cap. She put it on, stuffing shoulder-length dark blonde hair into it until not a scrap was visible. From a chocolate box she gathered up a handful of soil, which she rubbed into her face, neck and hands. Soulful bluey-grey eyes and good skin despite the appalling diet made Ilse too noticeable in public. On excursions such as these, often far from assistance, she preferred to look like a labourer and not too obviously female.

Downstairs Mutti was frowning in concentration at the kitchen table.

'Hello, darling. I thought you might be going today. I've got some things together.' On the hacked-about kitchen table were a silver photograph frame, two children's jackets knitted by Tante Frieda with wool unravelled from one of Vati's gardening jumpers, a blue and grey beer mug with lid and handle – one of a pair, the other having already gone – and a bracelet.

'No, Mutti, you can't. Not that,' gasped Ilse when she saw the gold bracelet that had been passed on to Mutti by Ilse's grandmother. 'I can't think of you without it.'

'We have no choice.' In her calm way Ilse's mother made light of the situation. 'Don't use it unless they won't take the other things. Put it somewhere safe.'

Ilse glanced down at her boot. 'What time did Michelle leave?'

'Sometime after seven. She went with your father.'

'How was she?'

Mutti shook her head. Ilse packed her rucksack. It was stained with living; a symbol of her life-style, as Michelle's medical bag was of hers. Sitting on the high stool by the sink she sipped a last drink with her mother. They were out of tea so instead she drank a brew made from dried strawberry leaves.

'*Auf Wiedersehen.*' Ilse kissed her mother.

From the verandah Frau Weinacht watched her daughter climb the track. Before she disappeared from view Ilse always turned to wave. It was a moment of tension. Who knew what would happen that day?

Once these woods had been benevolent and beautiful; a place for family outings and romantic walks. Now life-threatening things lurked under their canopy. The forest was in Ilse's blood. For as far back as she could remember it had always been there. Not a single one of its moods escaped her notice. Some days it warned her and she was extra cautious.

Heavy-booted and moving slowly she climbed the rutted track that led to the top of the ridge, along which ran a path that would take her to her port of call. For a while it passed grand entrances to houses, long winding mysterious channels that led to opulence; then it grew wilder and lonelier.

The final stretch to the top was tough. Her leg muscles tautened in agony as her boots found no hold on the loose shifting stones. At last she scrabbled onto the bridle-path along the summit and flopped exhaustedly under a bush. Her neglected stomach supplied no energy. Although young, the prolonged undernourishment had blunted her physical capabilities and concentration. Only their job rewards and Tante Frieda's garden produce kept the watery swelling of oedema at bay.

Thank goodness her rotting turnip pile was still there. When it had first appeared and why the good ones were not used she did not know. The bounty seemed to be all hers. At least there would be turnip for supper. The man-made vegetable mountain sat in majestic isolation above the deep railway cutting and snug against a wire-mesh fence. The cart-track snaked alongside. To the east the land fell sharply to the left and down to the sunless track, with the fir forest flanking on the right.

She never went directly to the turnips but stayed under a bush until her tortured breathing quietened and she could listen. No bird-calls today. Sometimes she had no choice as to which part of the day she came. Twilight was the worst: the owl hoots and the treachery of the dark. She shuddered as she thought about it, and wondered what the owl had made of that night when Liga must surely have lit up the whole of Europe. She was definitely a morning person. Situations seemed so much easier to deal with at that time.

Her ears strained to pick up sounds. Bush movements, workers' voices from the railway line, gunshots, heavy breathing or screams. This last sound, like a baby crying in the night or a dog whimpering to go out, penetrated into the nervous system, putting the body on red alert for unnaturally long periods of time.

She allowed half an hour, after which time she reckoned any concealed life would have lost patience, challenged her or made their own sounds. Bent double, her rucksack bumping on her back, she looked like a hunchback as she sped, furtively glancing, to her goal. Nimbly removing some of the vegetables, she gently eased away a makeshift plywood door. Lugging her bag behind her, she crawled into the hidey-hole that was carved out within and supported with stakes from the forest. Replacing the camouflage she lay down in the womb-like safety of the turnip-walled cave.

Not a moment too soon. Voices. Men. From below. She peered through her spyhole. Workmen on the line was not an unusual occurrence. They never looked upwards or picked up any vibrations of being watched. Today she could see six of them, very shabbily dressed in old uniforms and boots that looked as though they did not fit. In the country, devoid of competing noises, their voices carried well. At least it was German being spoken. Her own tribe. How beaten they looked as they bent to examine the buckled sleepers. Something dark lay across the line. She hoped it wasn't an unexploded bomb discarded by the pilots on their homeward trip. Certainly the men didn't want to touch it. She panicked when one of the men started climbing the bank towards her. Then she saw he was searching for a stick. Finding what he wanted, he returned to his mates. They prodded the object. It was a body. She was horrified. Not at the body but at how unmoved she was. Was she becoming too hard? What did survival cost you in humanity? Those who came through: what sort of people would they be? What would be their effect on their children? Would they even want to bring children into such a world?

The Germans talked a while. There was much shaking of heads. With boots and sticks they rolled the corpse away from the line, then covered it with stones. One of the men looked so familiar she was sure she had seen him before. The sight in her left eye wasn't that good so maybe she was wrong. Shuffling unenthusiastically, the group left for the city.

Today no trains had passed by. The line was still blocked, probably. She'd seen them on other visits though. Nothing but cattle-trucks with evil slit windows. There were people inside. She knew that because their arms dangled out as if beckoning for help. She shuddered. One heard things. Once a door slid open and something was bundled out. After the train had gone, fetid straw and other things covered the line.

After fitting the plywood door – another item jettisoned from passing trains – and piling extra rotten turnips against it, she took a gigantic leap, landing square in the middle of the pathway. Even long-jump champion at school had its uses!

The athleticism was necessary to ensure a track of trampled grass did not lead the curious directly to the entrance of her second home. With a handful of weeds and greenery she scuffed away the collection of footprints and planted a trail pattern that would lead any followers straight past her haven. The exposure of the roadway made her nervous, so she kept strictly within the tree-line until she came to the usual notice.

BEWARE – WOLVES

She knew they were probably more frightened of her than she was of them, but their sound bit into the soul. A no-hope melancholy cry that carried too clearly on the wind. Another reason she preferred morning forays. She knew precisely where the climbable trees were – just in case; and she might need them for something worse than wolves.

9

As the trees thinned she could see her place of business far below. Dorfshof was a mixed farm, comprising cattle, hens and crops. In charge was an elderly farmer, Herr Bertold, assisted by his wife and grown-up daughter. It was the latter who was Ilse's contact. Maria, an old classmate, was one of a multitude of women who were neither single nor married. Her husband was missing on the eastern front, presumed dead. Their child, Yvonne, ran around the farm, helping and hindering wherever she could. For her the world was still a place to have fun in.

Crouching softly, her knee sinking into the brown spindles of the pine-needled forest floor, Ilse scanned everywhere from her high-ground eyrie. She was looking for visitors: the SS searching out deserters or collecting people on their endless wanted list. One tiny indiscretion and you too went on this notorious list. Thereafter followed a period when every knock on the door held terror. Usually it came in the early hours of the morning when the human body is at its lowest ebb and when the activities of the secret police would be likely to attract the least attention.

Herr Bertold crossed the yard, his back perilously bent under the weight of a hay bale. All appeared normal. Cautiously she slithered down the bank, darting behind an outbuilding.

'Psst,' she hissed towards the open half-door of the kitchen. This was their way of calling for attention – a sort of code. If some undesirable element lurked, this sound could easily get drowned in the general clatter of the farmyard and the hissing of the flock of geese that formed their local neighbourhood watch service. Only Maria, sensitized to the farming hubbub she had known all her life, picked it out of the general mêlée.

'Ilse,' cried Maria in delight and relief.

'Oh my God, we wondered. . . . We knew, of course. Bright as day here. Even on full moon it's never been like that.' She raced across the yard, wiping her hands on a rubbery apron as she ran. They hugged.

'How are you, love? We've been so worried. We've had no news. Bits of things have been flying around and the cows have got eye infections.'

'I'm OK, thanks,' said Ilse with amazing understatement. 'What about you? The family? I saw your father hard at work.'

'We struggle on, hand-to-mouth survival as always,' smiled Maria ruefully. Ilse followed her into the kitchen, where she wriggled out from the straps of her bag. This was the hub of the household. The entire Bertold history must have taken place around this gargantuan table. Family members were born and died around it, on it or under it. It was such a long and huge piece of furniture that Ilse was sure the farmhouse had been built around it. No normal door could deal with the entrance and exit of the many-legged monster. It stood on large squares of ochre-coloured tiles. Underneath curled various sizes and breeds of cats and dogs, and even a pet rabbit. As usual, succulent simmering sounds came from the solid-fuel stove that spanned the length of a whole wall. This room was how Ilse pictured heaven. She hoped she would end her days in such a place.

'I've brought those knitted jackets you wanted,' said Ilse, still marvelling at her luck that an old friend had a child who needed the clothes her family were skilled at making. Before Maria could reply, a tiny blonde tub of energy tornadoed into the room.

'Tante Ilse, Tante Ilse,' she sang, pumping her grown-up friend's hand up and down, then dragging her towards the table. The child motioned to Ilse to bend down. She wanted to show off her new white rabbit.

'Oh I say,' said Ilse, bending to admire. 'He's beautiful. *Is* it a he or a she?'

'It's a mummy one. I'll have more and more, won't I? A whole family.' Yvonne's chubby arms reached to gather up the new love of her life.

'Look, Yvonne, I've brought a friend for Mummy Rabbit.' From the front pocket of her rucksack Ilse drew out a seated rabbit. It had been carved in the Bavarian woods by craftsmen. Her fellow rabbit-lover's face lit up with excitement.

'Pretty, pretty,' she bubbled, crawling under the table to introduce Mummy Rabbit to the new arrival.

Ample-bosomed in a buttonless blouse, Frau Bertold came in with a basket of eggs. Though toughened from farm work and dressed in old clothes, she carried with her an aura of glamour. Perhaps it was the mystique of her past life as an international singer. She had married late, apparently not unhappy to jack in show business pressure and redirect her professionalism into a more rural way of life. A woman to be admired. Ilse thought so anyway, and kissed her on the cheek.

'Hello, Ilse,' she smiled in welcome. 'You weren't?'
'I was,' replied Ilse. 'Hell on earth.'
'And your family?'
'All safe. The fire didn't get that far.'

'We haven't known what to think. We wanted to help but we can't leave the animals for long.' Frau Bertold sat down heavily and began stirring the soup. 'Onion all right?'

'Worn-out-car-tyre soup would be all right.' Ilse sat as near as possible to the delicious aroma that streamed out of the pot. Maria's mother was a woman of few words. She waited for information to be offered rather than asked for it.

'I was running for the basements. Most of those who went there died. Yesterday it was still too hot to reach some parts. Nearby a doctor was on duty. She shouted for me to follow. Thank God I did. Vati would normally have been working there at that time. It so happened it was his night off.'

Frau Bertold stopped stirring. Thoughtfully she said, 'God moves in mysterious ways. He doesn't always give us what we want but he gives us what we need when we need it.' Her mind seemed a long way off. Another time? A person perhaps? Although Ilse appeared to have momentarily lost her audience she carried on.

'Michelle — that's the doctor I was telling you about — is staying with us. She doesn't know whether her mother is alive. We've also got the head nurse, Katja Reinhardt. She's taken it badly. She always seemed so strong and yet when the crisis came she went off her head.'

'Often the way. Reinhardt, Reinhardt. Couldn't be the same, I suppose. Common name. There was one in the class above, though I don't know if she was a Katja. Bit of a bully.'

'Hmm, sounds like her. She really had it in for me. Now she's like a child.'

'Takes all sorts,' said Frau Bertold philosophically. She patted Ilse's hand. 'Here, have your soup. You're one of the lucky ones. A night I think when God's back was turned.'

A dishevelled Yvonne and her mother crawled from under the mighty table, where they had been delegates at a Rabbit Conference. Yvonne's lips pouted miserably.

'Tante Ilse, Mummy Rabbit and New Rabbit aren't making friends.'

'They will, sweetie. Don't you worry. Friendship just takes time. You can't rush it,' said Ilse between spoonfuls.

'How long?' persisted Yvonne.

'You never can tell. Both rabbits have been well-brought-up. I've sure they'll make it work,' smiled her older friend.

'These are adorable. Your auntie's handiwork?' Maria unfolded one of the woollen jackets, spreading it out on the table. Wonderingly she ran her hands over the garment. 'I wish I could do things like this,' she sighed.

Silently Ilse gave fervent thanks she could not, and wondered how much they would be worth in food.

'For me, Mummy?' asked Yvonne hopefully.

'Of course, silly. Who else would they fit?'

'I'll check what his lordship's got to spare in the food department,' said Frau Bertold. The way she left a room always made Ilse think of stage directions, 'Exit left with imperious flourish'.

Frau Bertold made several entrances carrying a collection of bags which she stacked on the table; half a dozen potatoes, two onions, six eggs and a jug of milk, which Ilse transferred into the two containers she had brought with her. Hardly a feast for a six-person household, but she well knew the black-market prices for such items – if you could get them. As they were friends, haggling was out of the question. If she thought she was short-changed there were others ways of balancing things out.

'Do I look grown-up? I could go dancing, couldn't I?' Yvonne whirled around the kitchen in her pale blue jacket.

'You could, sweetheart, and you'd be the prettiest one there.' The child clambered onto Tante Ilse's lap.

'You eat very fast.'

'I'm hungry,' said Ilse. Fortunately the child didn't yet know about supply and demand and the problems when the latter exceeded the former.

'I'd better go. I don't like the woods after dark,' she said over Yvonne's bobbing head. The silence was awkward. Uppermost these days was the thought: would this visit be the last one?

From the top of the bank she turned to wave to the three generations of women grouped outside their family home. They looked so small and vulnerable. How fragile it all was. Something happened and then the unseen part of a human being was borne away on the wind, living on only as long as those who missed them survived.

Against the sighs in the distance and the evening sounds she knelt down by a disused rabbit hole.

'Good girl,' she said softly. One by one she drew out five eggs. Only she knew of this particular hen's preference for country laying. Under moaning tree-tops and strange flutterings of wings she scurried home, anxious to see Michelle.

10

No one was home. Adult though she was, Ilse never became immune to the desolation at coming back to an empty house. No, she was wrong. Someone was home. Technically speaking, anyway.

'Will you tell Mutti I'm back and I've gone to bed?' There was no response. Not a flicker. Katja laboriously finished a row of knitting. Tante Frieda had commandeered her as an apprentice to the family's woollens industry. Ilse repeated her request.

'Yes, yes,' said the woman irritably. Ilse shrugged. Weak from her journey home, she went up the stairs on all fours. She left the black-out blind. No energy left. Slumping onto the bed, she slept far into the night.

The moon shone into the bedroom like a spotlight encircling actors on a stage. Michelle, an immobile grey statue, sat hunch-shouldered on the end of the bed. As though a malfunctioning clock was having trouble with its ticks, a constant *clink clink* penetrated Ilse's slowly awakening mind. The eyes of the statue were fixed on the blank wall. Its fingers, seeming disassociated from the brain, moved the black keys one by one round the key-ring.

Wriggling out of her chrysalis-like enclosure, Ilse sloughed off the bedding. She wrapped the old fur coat around Michelle's shoulders. The moon shifted almost from view. Now only a sliver shafted across the floor.

Holding up a half-melted key and in a voice that hardly reached her mouth, Michelle said, 'Our back door. Front door. Deed box. Filing cabinet. And this little one. My five-year diary. Mummy promised to keep it safe for me.' As Michelle's body relaxed into grief, there was an explosion as the pile of keys hit the linoleum. As the first convulsion of tears came, Ilse held her tightly.

'They tried to shoot me,' she sobbed. 'There were guards at the end of our road. Your Vati risked his life trying to stop them. Ilse, it's my mother, my home, and they wouldn't let me near.' Ilse had no words. Often she had held dying soldiers in her arms when they cried for their mothers. The experience was no use. This was too different. The pain felt like her own.

Gently she coaxed Michelle's head onto the pillow packing the bedding round her, only to have Michelle fling it aside as she searched under the bed for the lost keys. Finding them at last, she swept them up, clinging to them as if to the last link with her old life.

'And is that all there is?' she said too quietly. She turned away, then like a wounded animal curled herself into a ball. When Ilse touched her she was as stiff as a corpse.

The weeks following Armageddon were dreary and barren of hope, save for the green miracles of shoots that forced their way through blackened ground in once-upon-a-time gardens and the odd flowering shrub that lit colour-starved lives. The buildings' naked rooflessness received early spring rain. The living eked out existences in holes fashioned out of the rubble or herded into tiny evil-smelling basements. They haunted the city like rarely seen underground animals, seldom straying far from their territory and predominantly after nightfall.

It was a false dawn that came to Liga. Tentacles of terror were spreading from the east. Excruciatingly slowly the pincers of power encircled the city, then tightened. Rumours of atrocities that snowballed with each telling preceded the scourge. The stories fed like a cancer on the people's already unbalanced minds. Raids, starvation, insanitary conditions and multiple bereavements had pared their resistance away. Old men and women, Hitler Youth who had lost their idealism and the army of Mädchen in their teens and twenties were all that stood between the Red Army's swathe through to the west.

Each morning their prayers were for silence and deliverance. Each morning the gun-fire was louder. Many had suffered enough and chose their own methods of not having to face the invaders.

The extended Weinacht family welded into a fighting unit. Each had their function, each made their contribution, even Katja Reinhardt, who under the calming influence of Tante Frieda was now just irritatingly simply-minded. It was the anticipation of the violence against their homes and bodies that drove people crazy.

'The soldiers haven't been home for years,' Katja would mutter darkly.

Michelle's bereavement process took moody and unpredictable turns. It was hard to reach her. She buried herself in work. On the few occasions she came home, occasionally she loosened up enough to talk to Ilse.

'The propaganda department wouldn't want the general public to see these casualties. It wouldn't be good for morale. That's why they come in on the night goods trains.'

'Why haven't I seen them?' asked Ilse.

'My God, I'm glad you haven't. It's no place even for the hardened professionals. Ilse, they're so young. Not even time to grow a moustache.'

It was long after sundown in the unheated bedroom. Their nearness warmed and shut out reality for a few precious hours. Ilse shuddered. It was not from the night-time temperature drop, rather the soul shivering with foreboding.

'Can you save many?' she asked.

'My supplies are a joke. All we can do is bathe them, make them comfortable and treat their lice. We've got bandages and antiseptic ointments but I've no drugs for their pain. I have to amputate. Often. they come in with everything: typhus, dysentery, gangrene, water on the leg, frost-bite. You name it, they've got it. Even Asiatic VD, which makes you swell like an elephant.'

Ilse grabbed the fur coat just in time to stop it sliding off the bed onto the floor. 'And still they march to the front. It seems another lifetime ago when we cheered them off. I still haven't heard what happened to Outer. How magnificent they looked then! I've never heard. . . . Now our despatch rider's been called up. He can't be more than. . . .'

Ilse found she was talking to herself. Michelle was always tired, from long hours in squalor. She never looked peaceful when she slept, her forehead always puckered with worry as though some problem would never be resolved.

Next morning the household was up early. As usual Michelle had gone. Entombed in work mode she seemed like a prisoner within her own skin. Katja sat quietly in the corner kitchen seat, still encased in the pink quilted housecoat.

'They're coming,' she said quietly when she saw Ilse. Sometimes she would grab Ilse so tightly on the arm that the blood would stop.

'It'll be some time. Don't worry,' replied Ilse calmly. Would it, though? It was as if life was taking place in Technicolor somewhere else and would reach them soon but nobody knew when.

Mutti was by the sink staring hard at six small seed potatoes.

'If you stand there long enough they'll start sprouting,' laughed Ilse, planting a good morning kiss on her mother's cheek.

'Funnily enough, that's just what I was wondering. Do we eat them now or grow some more?' She looked at the hungry faces of her daughter, her sister-in-law and their guest. 'Eat them now, I think.'

Then she realized her daughter was not in her Red Cross outfit. Instead she wore her excursion clothes.

'Don't go today, Ilse. We can manage.' Frau Weinacht's face was tight, as though folded away, the emotions not for public display, even for her family. Heavily she sat down at the table. Her daughter put a hand on her shoulder.

'But Mutti, it might be our last chance. Maria promised me lamb. Anyway, the baker says they're days away yet. You said so yourself. Come on, Mutti, let's have one of your smiles. I'll be back long before dark.'

But Mutti couldn't smile.

'She's right, Ursula,' said Tante Frieda. 'You know what rumours are. I hear they're well-educated and disciplined. Go on,' she said to her niece.

'They're animals. I know,' burst out Katja.

'Shut up,' said Ursula Weinacht sharply, and went to look out of the back door so they couldn't see her face.

The usual rush of adrenalin that preceded these adventures was missing as Ilse turned to wave to the tiny figure of her mother at the back gate before she plunged into the forest to begin the first leg of her food mission.

11

The turnip depot, outlined against a horrible purple and orange horizon, was undisturbed. A colossal storm was in its first mutterings. She reached Maria's farm before the patter of rain turned to a white sheet of water. As their usual warning signal would not be heard above the noise of the storm, she dashed straight in.

Yvonne, her legs flailing endearingly in all directions like those of a new puppy, rushed into the kitchen to greet her.

'More rabbits, Tante Ilse?' She jumped up and down, pointing hopefully to the rucksack.

'Of course. When you grow up we're going into business together, aren't we – breeding rabbits?'

'Ooh yes.' The ritual of introducing the new arrivals to the present inmates of the nether regions of the table was gone through, to the entire satisfaction of rabbit breeder and supplier.

Maria flicked back her long black hair, shooed a marmalade cat off a chair, plumped up the squashed cushion, and didn't give the usual smile.

'What is it?' asked Ilse, sitting on the vacated chair.

'Nothing. Not my best day, that's all.'

'Come on, we've known each other too long. When you don't look at me, something's up.'

'Ilse, don't stay too long,' said Maria in a rush. She

suddenly got very busy at the sink. In a second Ilse was up from her chair and by Maria's side. She didn't say anything, just opened her eyes wide in a questioning look. Maria's eyes were frightened; she was trying to tell Ilse something, and Ilse wanted to run away. Lightning filled the room. It seemed to inject an evil chemical into the atmosphere, then above the roll of thunder there came a violent smashing against the door.

'Open up or we'll break the door down,' bawled a rough voice.

'Come on, we know you're in there. We've been watching.' Ilse recognized the dreaded language. Submerging her instinct for flight she sat down again by the stove. Stuffing the day's supply of baby clothes underneath her coat, so as to look bulky and maternal, she swept Yvonne onto her lap and began cooing soothing nonsense into her ear.

'Who's there?' shouted Herr Bertold from the stone sink in the adjacent scullery where he had been washing his hands.

'We'll have to,' hissed Frau Bertold to her husband. Ever since Ilse had arrived she had been hovering uneasily from room to room. Her husband grabbed her arm.

'They've only heard my voice,' he said frantically. 'Go up to the attic. All of you. Pull the ladder up after you.' Like the climax of an orchestral piece, the thunder and the invaders' hammering cascaded into one another. 'You too,' he urged Ilse.

'No, I'll risk it here.'

Maria stretched out her hand for Yvonne to take.

'No,' whispered Ilse urgently. 'She'll make a noise and give you away. They don't harm kids. They never harm kids. Go on. Don't worry.'

51

The enemy at the door would wait no longer. The wooden planks were bulging as heavy implements were repeatedly battered against it. Herr Bertold opened up the top portion. A boot kicked in the bottom half. The room darkened, then yellow and blue danced before their eyes as forked lightning sped to the ground behind five men. Ilse felt their menace coming at her in waves. With all the acting ability she could muster she willed these Red Army soldiers to believe in her bovine maternal role. They wore tin helmets and jodhpurs, and reeked of horses, sweat and ill will. Rifle poised, the bow-legged leader strode across the room. He yanked open the larder door.

'Nice little hoard. Empty it.' He motioned to his men to get cracking, then pointed his rifle at Ilse.

'The wife?' he asked Herr Bertold. He took the farmer's silence as a yes.

'Ugly.' He didn't waste his time with the soil-stained, lumpy peasant by the stove. He chucked Yvonne under the chin then produced a sweet, which the child consumed greedily. Sweets were a rare thing round these parts. She looked for more but the pack leader had other priorities.

'Search the place. Cellars, attics, the lot. You find anything useful – load it up.' Instantly the men obeyed his command.

Ilse and the farmer were like fossils. Not a muscle flinched. Even the child fell under the spell of fear. One of the minions stayed by the door, glowering. It was difficult to imagine that face ever smiling.

After the receding thunder there came other sounds. Raised voices. Scuffling. Doors banging. A fight on the stairs. Herr Bertold ran to the door. The soldier rammed him back with the sidebelly of the rifle. Stunned, the farmer tottered backwards to the chair. Moaning, he bowed his head and covered his ears with his hands. Screams came from the woods as one human being used his power over another. The anguish went on and on as if a power drill was penetrating deep into Ilse's head. Clawing. Sobbing. Subsiding. Shots. Silence. Feet tramping, growing fainter. Not meeting their eyes, the sentry melted away from the doorway.

The child played with Ilse's coat buttons, but Ilse's gaze was fixed on the floor. She noticed how neatly the tiles had been grouted. Numbed, as though she had been deep-frozen for a long time, she was barely aware of Herr Bertold lifting Yvonne from her arms. They might be back. . . . Then the urgency for flight overpowered her.

The next thing she knew she was hurling herself up the muddy bank desperately searching for footholes and scared witless at the thought of who was lying in wait in the dark humid forest. Bent double to dodge the low branches, her tears streaming down with the rain, she ran wildly. Again and again the forked lightning plunged into the earth.

'Kill me then,' she screamed at God. Dirty and spent and calling on the final spurt of energy, she dug furiously like a terrier and crawled into the turnip heap. The night and her spirit closed down.

'I don't want to live,' she said, her mouth pressed into last summer's bracken.

Quagmire was victorious over vehicles as mud oozed way above axle height. When the bitter Eastern European winter struck, the hoped-for mobility never arrived as machines' lubricants and innards turned to ice. When the German infantry had tried to penetrate Russia, they asked over and over again, 'Is there no end to this country?' and the vastness of Soviet territory banged another nail in their coffin. Supplies never reached them over those great stretches of godlessness. The only growth industry was in corpses at the rate of a thousand a day. It was patently obvious the Germans on the eastern front had been overrun, and a barely conscious Ilse was in the best position to verify history's other claim – the colossal size of the Red Army.

The retreated thunder left a forest heavy with moisture. Millions of leaves tipped surplus water onto the needle carpet begun in prehistoric times. Ilse raised her fever-flushed head to the sound of suckings and squelchings, metallic clinks, heavy clanks, leather slapping bodies, laborious blowing from hard-working nostrils. She knew, of course. Seemingly unending columns of horseflesh, manpower and armaments were moving west.

Then Ilse heard the now too familiar words used by the military when in sight of food.

'Load 'em up,' said an uneducated voice. From his further rapid speech Ilse deduced he had little knowledge of the correct use of verb tenses. She knew that much about the Russian language. A supporting prop of her den shifted. She waited for the inevitable discovery, every muscle on starting blocks, ready for the run. She'd opted for being shot in the back rather than the alternative of capture and rape.

Sounds of spitting juices, slushiness as a soft surface yielded, a swear-word, an exclamation of disgust.

'Yuk, full of maggots.'

The turnip mound lived on in rotten splendour. A smouldering cigarette was tossed onto nearby grass. It fizzed strongly, but thank goodness the dampness of the grass meant its life was short.

The weary day wound on. Ilse's body passed from semi-consciousness to red alert and back again. Surely by now Russia's entire military personnel must have passed by. The voices were raucous, the reprimands often accompanied by violence and scuffles, and the lascivious laughter that followed certain remarks made it clear the jokes were dirty.

Some way to the west, they seemed to be settling down for the night. Someone was playing a piano – beautifully. Ilse wondered whether they had their own tuner along with them. Then came sweet mournful singing and instrument-playing galore. Had the city's symphony orchestra come out here to entertain them? And someone had a great talent for the mouth-organ. In the small circle that served as her spyhole, a monkey decked in red harness came into view. It sniffed curiously, its nose twitchingly asking questions. Fortunately it had reached the limit of its rein. There was a quick yank and the monkey was gone. Ilse was full of disbelief. She must be dreaming. Monkeys and soldiers? And the Russian carnival wasn't yet over. The act that followed was the cow, goat and hen brigade.

It was long after dark before Ilse and the wildlife got their space back. She could hear their partying, and lay still in case there were scouting groups nearby. Her head was heavy, as though she was being swung up and down on a see-saw. Time lost all meaning. She never knew how many hours or days she lay there, passing through various stages of consciousness.

There seemed to be a peculiar amount of grunts, heavy breathing, digging, thuds, swishes – like soil dropping onto a coffin – and matches being struck. What the hell were they doing? Burying their dead? All this, it would appear, was taking place on the other side of the cart-track, out of sight of Ilse's viewing hole, where the land dropped steeply onto a series of plateaus and trees clung precariously, growing almost horizontally.

A fog closed over her brain as she sank into the sleep of a sick animal during which nature makes the decision: healing or death.

A small animal was foraging. It would scratch furiously, then stop. She could almost see its head on one side as it listened. It was a comforting noise; evidence she wasn't all alone, her space and survival fight were shared with another. Whatever it was gave off friendly vibes. Perhaps she was still dreaming? Her head felt a little easier but breathing was painful and her body burned as though someone had laid red-hot bars over her.

And then she screamed. Batting wings rushed through pine-tops. An owl screeched somewhere. A hand dangled through an opening.

'Ilse, thank God,' said the most beautiful voice in all the world. An ancient leather bag followed the hand into the den. Arms cradled her head as she was propped up to allow some liquid to flow down her throat. Then Ilse slid down a golden waterfall towards rest.

Without calendars and watches, neither knew how long the fever raged. Bottom first, Michelle backed into their home, raking in behind her the pile of hay she had obtained unofficially from the Bertolds' barn. Naturally she didn't tell Ilse where it had come from. Her friend would not elaborate about what had happened at the farm. Over the next few days, with the help of the hay padding and her own body heat, she beat off the threat of pneumonia from Ilse's weakened body.

'What time is it?' asked Ilse, speaking her first full sentence for days.

'Good question. Judging by the number of watches strapped to the arms of the Russians, I guess it'll be some time before we Germans know whether it's Easter or Christmas.'

Ilse raised her eyebrows.

'I had to cut a dozen watches off one soldier's arm before I could treat his wounds.'

'They didn't harm you then?'

'I was treating their sick. It gives you some immunity,' said Michelle casually. From a urine sample bottle she dripped water into Ilse's mouth. The water came from an animal trough in the corner of a nearby field. It contained every tick imaginable, but Michelle had crushed dandelion into it. This weed contained typhus-fighting properties. There was no choice but to risk the stagnant water until there was rain, by which time hopefully they would have found some means of collecting it. The terrain was high and the streams below too far away. Neither had the energy for the long climb down through sinisterly close pine trees, nor wished to risk encounters that would not be social.

'Dieter?' asked Ilse.

Michelle's face took on that hard look. 'Clearing cellars.'

Ilse raised a stick-thin arm. She touched Michelle's hair. 'If only there was something I could do.'

Michelle shook her head, momentarily closing her eyes. 'They're burning them. There are too many to bury. God, I hate war. Nobody escapes. It's like a pebble chucked into a pool: the ripples go on and on and on. It contaminates us all.'

Ilse lay still. She believed in miracles now. The familiar voice was gentle on her ears and sleep came. Abstractedly Michelle peeled bark from a twig, talking on, not realizing her listener had gone.

'You see, Ilse, the more I know, the less I know. Do you think that's the addiction, this mystery? Kids come into the profession straight from medical school. They drone on about the meaning of life, and I haven't the heart to tell them I haven't a single answer. You just do your inadequate bit, don't you?' She looked down at Ilse.

'You pig,' she said softly, 'you've gone and missed all my pearls of wisdom.' Michelle lay down under the interwoven pattern of the branch roof, pulling hay over her. They must conserve energy and sleep as much as possible. The city was cut off, the way ahead was blocked, there was nowhere to run. This was the beginning of a new career – displaced persons.

12

What a wild, dangerous woodland adventure it all was. Michelle's farming upbringing, combined with Ilse's local knowledge acquired during childhood games of cowboys and Indians, equalled survival. But two dominant characters living in close proximity meant clashes of personality were inevitable, and competition as to who could come up with the more inventive ideas was intense.

Michelle knew the various properties of roots, shoots, acorns and dandelions; Ilse knew where they could be found. The squirrels had forgotten where they had hidden their winter store but Ilse knew. Things like twine discarded by farms assumed monumental importance. Squirrel and jackdaw became delicacies on a par with oysters and caviar. The supple nature of hazel wands enabled Michelle to construct a cage. Suture thread combined with hours of patience meant that occasionally this rudimentary animal trap worked and they ate meat! Feeling extremely ill afterwards was a small price to pay.

As the danger to Ilse's health passed, she began to fret about home. When they heard sounds that worried them they penetrated deeper into the forest, seeking refuge in a disused badger set. To reduce the risk of discovery when at Done Turniping they built an extension. With the help of sticks sharpened by a scalpel, they dug a hole in the floor of the shelter. It was large enough to accommodate them both. When danger threatened – and so far there had only been false alarms – they dived into the dug-out, pulling branches and whatever greenery was in season over them. To an enemy force finding their lair it would be blatantly obvious someone had been living there, but it would appear the inmates had flown. A slim chance, but they took every precaution.

It was just before nightfall. They were in residence at the turnip mound and talking in low whispers.

'How long was I unconscious for? asked Ilse.

'I really don't know. I came out to look for you next morning. Your mother was very calm about it all. "She'll be at the farm with Maria," she said.' There were tears in Ilse's eyes. 'Surely I could have done something.'

'You saved a child from seeing something she might never have forgotten.'

'But don't you see? I didn't do it to save the child. I did it to save me.' Ilse's voice rose.

'I know they're friends of yours but I have to say they behaved stupidly. It was obvious they'd be found. They always find them. Damn it, Ilse, get rid of your hang-up over it. You're alive. You used your wits. You're around to perhaps help people in the future. You had no choice.' Michelle's tone was sometimes cryptic, sometimes soothing like a mother dealing with a perverse child.

'I don't know what time I found you. I had to hide in the woods for ages. Every bush seemed to rustle with something. I'll never forget those people. They were in a long line and all women. They sort of crouched as they ran. They looked as though they'd grabbed their Sunday best coat and they were lugging suitcases and small children. The eyes in those white faces will always haunt me. You could feel the panic steaming off them as their headscarves flapped, and they looked over their shoulders like foxes reckoning how close the pack is.'

They lapsed into silence until Ilse said, 'You missed the diggers then?'

'After the soldiers had gone there were digging sounds. I thought it must be bodies but I never heard any shots.'

'Where?' commanded Michelle.

Ilse waved a hand in the direction of the forest over the cart track.

'Come on, wonderwoman.'

'What now? It'll still be there in the morning.' Ilse felt drowsy. Not being in the least nocturnally inclined, she couldn't see the desperate hurry; but Michelle was burning up.

'Female curiosity, sweetheart, that's what. I'm consumed by it.'

Once over the track, they slid all the way down to the first plateau on their bottoms. Three sides of the flat area had rock walls. The floor was of bark and pine needles. It was not a place that would have many passers-by.

'Ah, evidence.' Michelle swooped to pick up a metal object. She held it up against the sky.

'Picture hanger. My grandfather had loads of them. This would carry a heavy one,' added Ilse, as she knelt, her hands sifting through the loose top surface.

'Watch it. Might be something pretty disgusting,' suggested Michelle, still turning the unexpected find over in her hand. She seemed rather preoccupied. 'Bit far from home wouldn't you say?' she mused thoughtfully.

Ilse hacked away with the heel of her boot. Michelle didn't join the physical labouring. She still seemed a long way off.

'Well, is madam going to help or not?' said Ilse rather tartly.

'Aha.' Michelle suddenly dived into the hollow which Ilse had scooped out.

'Damn,' cursed Michelle as she tried to tear the loosely woven mesh of the canvas. Foraging around the clearing she selected a sharp stone.

'This should do the trick.' She tore away the covering. There was dead silence for a long time as she contemplated what had been revealed.

'Well?' said Ilse, almost irritably. She would rather be sleeping.

'Manet,' breathed Michelle reverently. She sat cross-legged and unbelieving. She must have forgotten Ilse was there because she just sat scratching her ear and saying 'Manet' at regular intervals.

'How do you know?' asked Ilse, bending forward to get a closer look at the top portion of the painting showing below the ornate gold-decorated frame.

'I knew an artist once. He was studying here at the academy in Liga. He taught me a lot about art appreciation. He was obsessed with it. More than with me.' Michelle ended with a laugh.

There were several more wrapped items. Michelle then remembered she had her scalpel with her. Rolling down the top part of a malodorous sock, she pulled out the cloth-covered instrument. Unsheathing it she set to work on the other parcels. There were more paintings; beautiful, rich and startling in the sombre forest light.

'Degas, El Greco, if I'm not mistaken.' Michelle rocked back on her heels, covered the scalpel and placed it back beneath her boot top and sock.

'Nicked?' Ilse stood, hands on hips, at the side of the hole, her forehead puckered as she tried to piece the jigsaw puzzle together.

'Yes, nicked.'

'What the hell do we do about this?'

'Nothing,' said Michelle. 'What can we do?' Who's in power now? Nobody knows.'

'Our pension, d'you reckon?' Ilse started to giggle.

The opening scene of *Macbeth* couldn't have been weirder than the setting of this dungeon-like declivity. Two young women laughing uncontrollably and dancing around a cache of priceless oil-paintings against a backcloth of black forest above which flitted owls and bats.

'Our pension,' spluttered Michelle.

Today they were in residence at Done Turniping. Spring was fading and the woodland floor across the track was awash with wild flowers. As the sap rose higher in the trees so too did their urge to discuss the future.

'But I've got to risk going home sometime. They'll think I'm dead,' said Ilse petulantly, expecting resistance. She was leaning against the branch and vegetable wall, prising away caked mud from her boots. As she looked up at her friend, her eyes were defiant. She was fed up with Michelle's ultra-caution.

'And what if you do go back now? Your father might well end up dead,' replied Michelle acidly. On deeper acquaintanceship Ilse found out how severely practical Michelle could be, sometimes to the point of insensitivity. Michelle hammered her point home.

'For goodness' sake, Ilse, sometimes you don't think. If any of those soldiers lays a finger on you, do you really think your father's going to stand by and let them? You're mother's the wise one. She worked it out long ago. Your father doing his job and you on the road gives you both a better chance of survival.'

'Ok, Ok. You're right as usual. It makes me sick. You're always right.'

Michelle softened. 'I'm sorry. I didn't mean to have a go. It's just you tend to rush into things without thinking them through. I don't want any harm to come to you.'

'I know, I know. I need an anchor. Vati was the only one who could deal with me.'

Michelle continued scraping the maggot-riddled parts from the turnip. 'Yuk. When we get back to normal I don't think I can face one of these things again. I can see the menu now; *Vegetable of the day – swede*. Ugh. Normal life? *Will* anything ever be the same again? We talk about wars for decades afterwards. Why? Is it because it throws up the best in human courage, and degradation at the other end of the scale?' Michelle's eyes stared unseeing. Then she smiled at Ilse, her face returning to good humour. 'Look at me talking like a war veteran,' she laughed.

'Welcome back,' said Ilse.

'Seriously, though, how *do* we get word to your mother? There's got to be a way. I told her we'd probably have to lie low. Did she hear me, though? Katja was throwing a fit at the time.'

'She doesn't know you found me,' added Ilse quietly.

There was a physical ache around her heart. How much she had taken for granted. All the words she hadn't said. All the things she hadn't done for her parents. She'd been too busy with her social life to notice them growing older and to be aware of how much they loved her. Always thinking of her own life, never sparing a thought for how their lives were going.

As if reading her thoughts, Michelle stopped her culinary preparation. 'They do know, you know.'

'What do they know? said Ilse miserably.

'That you love them. It's part of nature. At a certain point you technically leave the nest to go your own way. You need that energy, that aggression, that almost arrogance in order to forge your way in a world that's indifferent to whether you're around or not.'

'You really think that?' Ilse fiddled distractedly with her rotting laces.

'Of course I do. Your parents know about the world. They're shrewd and they're kind, and what a combination! Come on, chin up. Tell me a naughty story.'

'I think we've exhausted all those. I can tell you a shaggy monkey story, though.'

'What?'

'I'd never have believed it. The Russians' progress was like a glorious circus with thousands of performers. Yes, I even saw a monkey.'

'Monkeys? Now you must have been hallucinating,' retorted Michelle.

'No, truly I saw a monkey. It was on a red velvet lead and it sniffed so close I could have touched it.'

'Hell, you're almost humanizing them. I'll be joining up soon.'

'They're beautiful musicians, anyway.'

'I think we're going a bit loopy.' Michelle shook her head.

'Come on, help with ideas. *What* are we going to do?'

Michelle wriggled back into her hay sleeping-bag and stared at the ceiling. She chewed a piece of straw.

Ilse was still enjoying winding Michelle up. 'Well, they do say you should play the hand of cards you have as best as you can. Let us consider what cards we hold. Homeless, apart from a roof over our heads courtesy of

Mother Nature. Jobless 'cos we'll get topped if we go back to them. Indifferent health, but I suppose we're alive. Oh yes, and we've got each other in between the arguments.'

'Sounds wonderful,' mumbled Michelle through the straw. 'How's your English?'

'Pretty passable. I studied it for years and learned English shorthand at college.'

'You know,' mused Michelle, 'we want a job with the English or the Americans. We've got to move west. But how? The Russians are ahead of us now.'

'Oh come on, Michelle, can you just see us at a job interview? "In our spring collection we present Ilse wearing the very latest in ripped wool. You will appreciate the well-ventilated sweaters and efficient zipless trousers. For real comfort in leisure activities this outfit is best worn without the benefit of undergarments. It is anticipated that this will be what the best-dressed refugees in Germany will be wearing this year."'

Ilse had managed at last to penetrate her friend's sombre mood, and Michelle took up the story.

'"The fashion pages of exclusive Sunday supplements are declaring that open-toed boots will be all the rage this season. Their versatility is undeniable, their openness allowing freedom of movement and exit vents for body odours which kill all household germs and will be available at most leading stores that stock the *Indescribable* collection."'

There were snorts and snuffles as they attempted to giggle quietly.

'Well,' managed Michelle when she had recovered enough to speak, 'seems we've no alternative but to deliver ourselves into the hands of kismet.'

'*Malsehen*, as Mutti would say. Time will tell. Goodnight.'

'Goodnight.'

A dangerous escape route presented itself quite unexpectedly.

13

'Mmmm, today really does feel like the first day of the rest of our life. Just look at that mysterious haze on the horizon. It makes you tingle. I really feel anything is possible.' Michelle stretched and brushed away the clinging bits of bedding. Another tousled head appeared beside her.

'The sun's awfully high. We've overslept. It makes me nervous when we do that. I mean, do we know whether we snore or talk in our sleep? What if someone's passing?'

'Well, I can put your mind at rest. You do snore,' said Michelle wickedly.

'How I hate you people who are so cheerful in the morning. And you, my dear, twitch. The number of times I've been whacked with your arm. You conduct the Liga Symphony Orchestra at nights.'

Michelle chose not to listen when it suited her purpose.

'It's a gift – this morning. Just look at that.'

The sun behind them was not yet shining above the trees onto Done Turniping, but it picked out the high ridge on the other side of the line. A herd of red deer grazed in a clearing. The sun slanted down as if through prisms of coloured light, making it seem that steam was rising from the animals. They felt they were looking at a scene older than biblical time.

'It's magic. Sometimes I don't want it to end.' Michelle leant against Ilse's shoulder as they looked at the peaceful deer.

'I know. Me too.'

Lush foliage had healed the damage inflicted by the passage of the Russian army, and it was difficult to hide the signs of their own habitation. There had to be trampled grass somewhere. They felt the longer they stayed the more they were increasing their chances of discovery. Neither had come up with a sensible idea. They had no information to go on. What was happening in the world? Where was it safe to go? They didn't know. They were totally out of touch.

'Quiet.' Michelle waved frantically at Ilse in a calming movement. The pores of their skin stood out like insects' antennae as they sought information from the noise. Voices sounded far down in the ravine-like cutting. Vainly they attempted a spot of rural net-curtain twitching but they couldn't see anybody. It was the 'desert island syndrome'. Desperately they wished to hail the ship that was passing, but was it a friendly flag that flew from its mast? Heavy boots bit into clinker. Silence. Stones kicked around. Silence. Muffled conversation. A long silence.

'Phew,' said Ilse, relaxing.

'German,' said Michelle, her face alight with hope. She crinkled up one eye as she peered through the piece of piping. The owners of the voices moved into her line of vision.

'Three of 'em,' reported Michelle. Then she began to sound like a horse-race commentator 'One of 'em bends down – points to something on the track – Man Two scratches his head – Man Two's voice is very familiar.' Then she shrieked so loudly that Ilse fell backwards.

'What the hell. . . .'

'It's Hans. Ilse, it's Hans.'

Michelle the Cautious was set upon dashing down there. Ilse held her back.

'Steady on there. We've lasted this long. How do we know who he's with?'

'Oh Ilse, come on. Look at them. Clapped-out clothes, holey boots. Do they look like superiors? Come on, let's risk it,' she pleaded.

'What have we got to lose? Someone's going to find us sometime,' and she followed her friend. They clambered over the wire fence, leaving most of their clothes attached to its strands.

'Hans. Hans,' screamed Michelle as she tore down the bank. Ilse could see the horror on the men's faces before they turned tail and ran. They'd got so used to each other, she and Michelle had forgotten what a pair of filthy old crones they must look. The men's running turned to shuffling and cowering as they sought cover behind bushes further down the line.

'Hans,' moaned Michelle, sinking to the ground, the sudden exercise racking her with pain. Now Ilse saw her in a different way: the huddled heap of rags, struggling to draw oxygen, the head heavy with grey, the end nodule of each bone seeming as though it must surely puncture the fabric of the skin. It couldn't end like this. She held her customary conversation with the sky and whoever was in charge up there.

'We're not going down. You just watch me.' Filling her lungs with air she yelled.

'Hans. It's Michelle and Ilse. Michelle. Michelle. Michelle.' She switched to the name he would most recognize and respond to. Summoning up her last energy she began to hobble towards the hiding men. One could hardly call it running. That was what she had done in her teens when she was in the school athletics team. She'd been heard. One man stood up. He stepped towards her. She hardly knew him, it was Michelle he'd known since she was four, but the relief of anyone familiar made her hurl herself into his arms.

'Ilse,' he said. Just before her face disappeared into the tobaccoey greatcoat she saw two sets of round eyes, one pair set above a bushy sandy moustache, the other peering from a grotesquely scarred face.

'Hans, get Michelle. I don't think she'll last much longer,' mumbled Ilse. Drained, she slid from him onto the bank. Holding one of her hands he gently assisted her to the ground. Still he said nothing. His face couldn't take it in. Then his huge limbs, like pistons on the wheels of the trains that used this line, galvanized into movement as he hurled himself towards Michelle.

Ilse's face was streaked and blotchy where she had rubbed her eyes too hard. She looked up to see a thin, sandy-haired man watching her. His face was kind. He was wringing his hands together as if desperate to help but not knowing how.

'Poor girl, poor girl,' he murmured over and over again. The man whose gruesome face had one eye higher than the other shared his anxious glances between Hans legging it up the track and Ilse flopped on the tussocky bank. All three looked east. They had to shield their eyes against the brightness of the morning sunlight.

The great hunk of a man was kneeling by Michelle. Gently he tipped her chin up so he could see her face better. He was talking to her. She looked towards the three of them. Grasping Hans' coat sleeve, she levered herself up. Together they negotiated the stumble-trap of a gully between sleeper and bank. Hans guided her in front of him, his hand under her elbow.

'Ernst,' said Hans indicating the kindly man. 'And Karl. Both from the coffee business. Your father got us this job.'

'I think you thought the demons were finally coming to get you,' said Ilse, 'but you don't seem surprised to see us. You've seen Vati?'

'We're not, and yes. Your mother told me which farm you usually went to. It was deserted, so we've been out checking around while working on this stretch of line. We thought you might need this –'

Before Hans could say any more Karl yelled to them, 'Down here,' and he flung himself against the girls.

They dived for bush cover as a massive roar split the morning. A train hurtled out of the tunnel, the cattle-trucks were loaded with singing soldiers. Some were swigging from bottles. Others took pot-shots at anything they felt like. Some debris was chucked out. A vodka bottle crashed against a nearby rock. Then they were gone, leaving the countryside as if a wound had bled open.

They lay in a heap under the close-growing bushes, stunned at their folly of standing out in the open.

'You'd think the war was over the way those men were going on. Anyone see their uniforms?' whispered Hans.

'Ukrainians,' said Karl. His face was a mass of bumpy weals. One of the eyes was useless. How long had he lain with his wounds unattended to? He must have read the look on Michelle's face.

'Fortunately, I don't have to look at it,' he laughed, 'and at least I'm still here.' It was the deep, calm voice of one who had been to the brink and was now grateful for small blessings.

'I wish I'd been there,' said Michelle simply.

Hans' greatcoat had endless pockets. Like a magician

producing a rabbit, he laid on the ground bread, sausage, sauerkraut. Each provision had been wrapped in twists of paper. His final flourish was a flask of real coffee.

'Don't ask,' he said as the two women fell upon the feast as convicts onto bars of gold.

'As I was saying when we were so rudely interrupted by our foreign guests, we thought you might need these.' He smiled as he watched the inelegance of their devouring, and glanced at his wrist. Realizing it was empty he then looked at the sun.

'You too?' enquired Michelle, noticing.

'It's years since I owned one. My brain's still locked into a nine-to-five mentality although the routine went ages ago. We're not very flexible creatures, are we?' Hans laughed.

If their stomachs hadn't been half empty and their nation in the grip of enemy forces, it could have been a picnic of their youth that now seemed as distant as if it belonged to other people. Hans leaned back against the woody stem of a shrub and told his story.

After the coffee warehouse burned to the ground, Hans and Ernst, his manager, had no employment. The Nazis put them to work clearing the cellars of the dead, while Ilse's father was overseeing the mammoth operation of getting Liga Station fully functional again. When the first Red Army regiment arrived, it was the Nazis who had most to fear. They were the scalps these Russians wanted. It was the ex-criminal, uneducated thugs who came along behind that terrorized the city with their looting and raping. Herr Weinacht's job was still necessary, for the Russians needed an efficient rail service. Hans and Ernst were useful as forced labour.

Michelle nodded. Usefulness meant survival.

One day Herr Weinacht arrived home to find his wife and sister-in-law sitting on a suitcase in the road outside their house. Some Russian officers had thrown them out – they needed the house as accommodation for high-ranking chiefs. Katja Reinhardt was dead; the sound of ever-nearer gunfire had driven her to the weed-killing concoction in the garden shed.

Ilse's father went to his new bosses, saying he could not work properly if his family was on the streets, and they rehoused them in a flat in a partially ruined house in one of the seedier districts of the city.

Karl was in one of the last train-loads of casualties to reach Liga from the eastern front before the city burned, his face disfigured by an exploding mine that had also killed his friend. But he was in the right place at the right time when Ilse's father was desperate for men to clear the tracks.

'You can't come back to Liga,' ended Hans. 'It's not safe for women and there's no food for Germans.'

'At least they're alive,' sighed Ilse, sinking back onto the ground and closing her eyes.

Michelle sat very still, her hands over her mouth, her forehead puckered, past memories and visions before her eyes.

At last she spoke.

'We've been asking ourselves "where next?"'

'Which is why we're here. Over to you, Ernst.' Hans nodded to his colleague to take the floor.

Beneath the quiet demeanour of this thinning-haired undermuscled man, one sensed efficiency. In lieu of a pencil he selected a twig. As a drawing-board he used the dark weedless soil. As he punctured its surface with their plan it gave off a scent like brackish aftershave. The five of them pored over the marks in the soil. Their lives hung on the success of this venture.

Ernst spoke low and quickly. Not a word was wasted.

'Adjacent to where we are now sitting we will place an obstruction across the line, so the train will have to stop. The distance between here and the tunnel should allow enough time for the driver to halt the train. The object will be soft, thus running no risk of derailment should the train fail to stop in time. We know there's a supplies train going west tomorrow morning. We also know it's at least thirty carriages. That means about a third of the train's length will still be under cover of the tunnel. We hide in the bushes that grow close to the tunnel's entrance. There's hardly room for a man to walk between the tunnel walls and the train, and if there is a guard at the rear we doubt he'll leave his post. If he does, we'll hear and clonk him.' Ernst pounded the air with a clenched fist.

'Do they lock goods carriages?' asked Michelle.

'Not usually. We'll have a crowbar with us just in case,' volunteered Karl. He had been sitting with his elbows resting on his raised knees. His boot-clad feet were splayed out. Ilse could see how dried out and cracked his footwear was. All five toes were visible from one of them where sole and upper had parted company. Thank goodness it was good weather.

'What's the train carrying?' asked Michelle.

'Grain, swedes, that sort of thing,' said Ernst.

Michelle hooted. 'Swedes! Good God, Ilse, did you hear that? Swedes!'

The men looked puzzled. Michelle explained.

'Turnips. We've slept on them, under them, eaten them, studied their infestations. There is nothing we can't tell you about the turnip.'

Ernst stayed serious. He produced five lengths of rubber hose. Michelle's eyebrows shot up.

'You might well have to sleep under turnips a little

while longer. These are for breathing if you have to submerge yourself completely.'

'You've thought of everything.' Ilse was full of admiration.

'It's risky. They're bound to stop along the way, dropping off supplies as the Reds advance. We don't know how far west the train will go. We don't know the stopping points. All we are certain of is that the Reds are moving fast and they need food. Because of the little information we have, the whole thing is extremely dangerous. You don't need me to tell you what they're doing to women. And us? If we don't get shot we'll be shipped somewhere inhospitable, and used as forced labour until we drop dead.' There was silence as Ernst doodled patterns in the soil. Michelle and Ilse looked at each other.

'I've no one to go back to and nothing more to lose,' answered Michelle.

'And I can't risk my parents' lives by going back,' Ilse joined in.

'We barely manage to find enough to eat. We can't pinch things now the farm's burned down,' added Michelle.

'You never told me,' said Ilse sharply.

'It wouldn't have done you any good to know at the time. Sorry.' Michelle looked uncomfortable, while Ilse looked distressed.

The men didn't influence their decision. They looked so beaten it was a wonder they could work. Their skin was a yellowy hue, highlighting the black circles around their eyes.

'We'll have to be getting back. We can't risk letting your father down. He's doing his damnedest convincing the Soviet authorities that we're indispensable railway technicians,' said Hans, anxiously peering down the empty line through a gap in the bushes.

'You'll be seeing Vati, Hans? Tell him I love them, that I'm OK and will be in touch as soon as I can.'

'I'll try, though now he's the man with the most knowledge of railway engineering, he's so busy and it's difficult to see him. His superiors were lost in the fire.'

'What time tomorrow and where?' asked Michelle briskly.

Ernst took charge again. 'Half past seven. Morning. Under cover of the bushes next to the tunnel-opening on this side of the line.'

'Something for your memoirs when you're little old dears,' grinned Hans.

'What a cheek. I intend to be glamourous to the end. What about you, Michelle?'

'I might spin out the glamour bit until next week.' Michelle's face belied the light-heartedness of her voice.

Karl didn't join in the general frivolity. 'What on earth have you two fed on?' he asked. Ilse was still feeling light-headed about the adventure and using her jocular mood to squeeze back the fear that was ebbing through her system.

'I suppose under "occupation" you'd have to put "pilferer". Though thinking about your question I suppose Michelle's been the "thief" and my job's been that of "poacher". I certainly understand why animals and birds sleep a lot and spend ages just listlessly sitting. It conserves your energy and you don't need so much food.'

It was difficult to know whether Karl was smiling. There was a slight tuck on the crinkled skin at the mouth corner.

'We'll try and bring some food for you tomorrow,' he said.

'Thank you, Karl.' Ilse looked at him with gratitude.

They all embraced. There was pain in the parting as though the fragile chain of comradeship would be broken by absence. The women crawled slowly up the bank to Done Turniping. They watched as the men shuffled bent-shouldered to the tunnel. One by one its darkness claimed them. It was the same one through which Ilse had fled home on the night of the bombing.

They spent a quiet evening at the badger set. A spell had been broken. They still yearned for the familiarity of the known but their minds had gone ahead to the future. Ilse looked around the soil walls so safe and deep.

'We've had to modernize, of course. Add an extension and one or two modern conveniences, but at least . . .'

'We had vacant possession,' finished Michelle. They lay quietly in their hay beds listening to the stillness. When almost asleep Ilse heard Michelle turn over and say softly, ''Bye Mum.'

'Sleep well,' said Ilse.

'Sleep well.' There was the comfort of a hand squeeze. Then sleep.

14

'When did you last go out on a proper date?' asked Michelle in a whisper as they made their way through the forest to the railway line.

Ilse crinkled her face in concentration as she gave deep thought to the question.

'About four years ago,' she said at last.

'Then we'd better not miss this one, Girl Friday,' giggled Michelle.

'Twit. I knew you were winding me up! It's too early for that. Give a girl time to charge her batteries. And watch it, I'm the one with money. Not so much of the subordinate status bit. You doctors like to play up your supposed mystique and power.'

'Just seeing what I can get away with. One dominant personality sparring with another makes life interesting,' joked Michelle.

'I think I prefer "quiet" to "interesting"', said Ilse as her skinny posterior disappeared into their vegetable hide. Inside, the atmosphere was like that of moving house. Their metaphorical suitcases were packed and waiting in the hallway. With twine they had tied their one piece of luggage to their waists in order to free their hands for all the physical activity involved in climbing, hiding and surviving.

'Hope my boots last,' said Ilse, fiddling with the string that wound round and round the toe part, keeping upper and sole together. She checked the heels. Mustn't lose those. She rubbed her hands together, then blew on them. Her breath billowed visibly in the chill of the early morning air. They took a final nostalgic look round, then at each other. Ilse's face was a mixture of doubt and good luck as she gave a thumbs-up signal. They were so near to their next stage every sound frightened them that at the last moment something might extinguish this faint flicker of freedom.

They crept and froze. Then crept and froze again down the scree of the man-made mountain. A weasel shot out of a hole, and Ilse thought her heart would pack in.

Amid the indignant shrieks of disturbed birds they reached cover. Breathing heavily, they crouched, listening. They trembled violently from fear of failure and from the cold; their meagre clothing lacked warmth. Some distance away there came the scrape of boot on stone. Michelle put her finger to her lips. Who you were expecting wasn't necessarily who you got. Gently Michelle parted the foliage and fixed her eyes on the darkness of the cavern's mouth. The scrunching reached deafening proportions as its echoes reverberated around the curved walls. Surely something terrible would shoot out. The sounds subsided as they reached daylight.

'OK,' said Hans' voice. Next moment they were joined by the flushed and heaving-shouldered men.

'Thank God,' said Michelle giving Hans' arm a light squeeze. 'The last bit of preparation's always the worst.'

The men were buttoned up to the neck like parcels in their railway company issue greatcoats. They were the lucky ones. A huge slice of the population owned no coat at all.

Ernst signalled to Karl to unluggage himself. On the

ground appeared food – this time substitute coffee – five lengths of hosepipe and two voluminous pairs of men's trousers.

'Do I take it then, Karl, that you are ashamed to be seen with us?' demanded Michelle seriously. Only Ilse recognized the single twitch of the top lip that meant her friend was building up to a leg-pull.

Karl looked embarrassed. 'No, I didn't mean anything like that.' He fidgeted in agitation at having done the wrong thing. Ilse noticed the gold wedding ring he had been wearing yesterday was gone. Was the price of two pairs of trousers one gold ring?

Michelle changed mood completely. 'I'm sorry, Karl. Ilse and I have got so used to sending each other up in order to cope with things that perhaps we've forgotten our manners and how to respond to kindness. We're desperate for these things, of course. Thank you so much,' and she hugged him.

Ilse burst out, 'Did you see Vati?'

'No but I got your message through. Don't worry, he knows,' said Karl.

'When you lot have sorted out your wardrobe perhaps you'd like to join me in a spot of sack filling,' commanded Hans, already doing a reconnaissance of the scene. 'Just you, Karl, and Ernst. Bring the sacks', he said, and was gone.

The women struggled into their new trousers.

'Do you think I've lost weight on the forest-food diet?' asked Ilse.

'Don't you start. I've already put my foot in it once. These trousers sure were made to accommodate a large beer gut,' said Michelle, making multiple folds of the trousers' waistband, slinging a piece of string around herself and knitting the whole caboodle together.

'We're a nation of stockingless women,' she added, looking at the miserable socks struck on the end of her legs. Then she folded together the remains of Ilse's trousers and her own skirt.

'Useful bandages,' she muttered, more to herself. Ilse was preoccupied watching what was going on in the distance.

'Wish they'd hurry up. It's getting seven o'clockish when the sun hits half-way up the opposite bank.' Ilse's right hand was clenched and white-knuckled as she held it to her mouth.

'Relax, love. I get the impression Ernst is a stickler for detail. I have full confidence he knows what he's about.'

'Mmm. . . .' replied Ilse.

Dark running figures came down the line. The shrub wall parted and the five were reunited. In silence they crouched, marble-like as athletes before the gun, these fugitives wanted no false starts.

A tiny tremor came from deep inside the earth. It grew and grew until their heads were splitting with the din. A volcano of air blasted leaf and branch and nature's detritus against their faces. Like a metal snake it roared out of the tunnel. There was a grind of tortured metal as brakes screeched and then the beautiful sound of a train slowing. Their prayers were answered. It stopped.

There was the urgency of running feet, then the sounds died away as the footsteps went towards the front of the train. Michelle and Ilse's eyes were fixed on Hans' face. 'Now?' their looks asked of him. Hans gave a slight shake of the head. He was right. An out-of-breath soldier from the rear of the train passed within an arm's reach of them. Ilse could smell the tobacco and unwashed clothing. They watched his pincer-toed progress as he joined his mates at the scene of the obstacle.

Hans jerked his head in a 'come on, team' movement. Crowbar first, he eased out of the bushes towards the carriage just inside the tunnel. No force was necessary. The truck door slid sweetly to reveal stacks of loose vegetables and tied sacks.

The slit-punctured cattle-trucks stood high off the ground. Karl cupped his hands to form a home-made stirrup. Michelle, then Ilse, placed a foot into the calloused human-mounting block, and were catapulted onto the squishy sack pile. The door closed, leaving them in semi-darkness. They heard the same sounds next door as the men took occupation of their berth.

Their breathing was loud and uneven from the tension. As an actress arrives early at the theatre in order to get the feel of the stage on which she will perform, wordlessly they took stock of their temporary shelter. At least they were spared more turnips. The pile in the corner, though, came from the same family. Michelle recognized it as mangel-wurzel, a type of cattle beet.

'Still got their travelling farm with them then,' whispered Ilse. No sooner were the words out then there came a splash of liquid on stones. The heavy boot noises moved away.

'Nature break,' said Michelle. They could feel each other's grins.

'Fancy,' she went on, 'and we hadn't said a thing for ages and he gets the urge right by our wagon. Not details one can plan for.'

'I can't stand being all shut up,' whispered Ilse.

'And I hate the dark,' finished Michelle.

Ilse nipped her nose with a finger, then buried her face in a coat lapel as she stifled a sneeze. Running-eyed she at last managed to speak.

'At least we're not asthmatic or paranoid about mice.' There was a minuscule plop and the feeling of tiny feet dancing over her legs.

'I guess we'll be tying up our trouser bottoms before we're through. We'll just have to learn to share. After all, they were here first. We'll burrow under that lot when the train starts moving.' Dimly Ilse could see Michelle indicating the mangel-wurzels.

The air in the wagon was tepid and tinged with rural odours. Ilse's jaw began to quiver uncontrollably.

'Oh Michelle, I've never been so scared. What if we don't pick up on the right sounds? What if we don't jump before the station? What if the doors won't open?' Ilse's voice was steadily rising.

'Come on, darling. Don't give in now. We've done all we can. It's up to the *liebe Gott* now.'

'Where on earth would we be if we hadn't met up,' sighed Ilse.

'Life would have been a whole lot drearier.' Michelle's voice was full of sadness. It was almost as if, faced with a future that might not exist, they savoured a second time the vivid images of comfort and comradeship from the past.

'You know, we didn't discuss telling the boys about the paintings. No one will know.'

'It crossed my mind too,' agreed Michelle, 'but then we don't know Ernst and Karl well enough. Perhaps we'll tell just Hans. See what he thinks. I guess the Soviets won't be long picking them up, and that'll be that.'

'Oh well, don't expect we'll last long enough to collect our pension.'

'Come on, pull yourself together. Positive thinking.' Michelle's tone was getting edgy. Why didn't the train start? What were they doing? Had they noticed something? Was there a search on?

The heat and flush from nerves and exertion receded. Their body temperatures dropped and they felt colder and clammier. The wood of the antiquated carriage creaked now and then. Suddenly there was a toppling sound ending in thud. Ilse stifled a scream as the topmost vegetable rolled down, landing at her feet. It had white marks where it had been gouged, and sat by her left foot, leering grotesquely like a carnival mask.

Then came a lurch so violent that Ilse was sure her heart hit the side of her rib-cage, then bounced to the other wall and back again. They fell against the sacks and stayed there during the jerking whilst wheel ground metal, the train gathered speed and their commitment was final.

They dragged away some of the beet, clearing a space between the wall and the heap. After secreting themselves in the opening they pulled vegetables and sacks over themselves. The rhythm of the engine music went on for a long time. It lulled them into the Land of Don't Care. They had underestimated how much fear and near-starvation had eroded their motivation. A stupor took control of their minds and bodies.

15

Ilse swam in the perfect beauty of those precious moments between sleeping and waking, a gift of time before the mind realizes the problems of the day. It was a space filled with frail, gentle singing, and yearning for parents, homeland and the past. Like fingers of water claiming a beach at neap-tide, the words drew her towards awakening.

Singing? They were at war. They were on a train. They were about to be discovered. *Singing*? Which arms and legs belonged to her? In the confined space she tried to move, but cramp took possession of her body in a series of agonizing contortions. Her teeth biting through her bottom lip, she fought against the need to cry out. As the pain receded, another panic arose. How cold Michelle was. Her hand was icy, like bone china. Was it the half-light or was she purplish-blue? It was the trick of the light.

'Ohhhhh. . . thank you, God,' she sighed as Michelle stirred with life.

'Singing?' said Michelle as she came round.

The doors ratcheted open and the truck was transformed with light. A swarm fastened onto the victuals. Undefended, they disappeared under the bellies of creatures with fiercely probing arms. They waved and jabbed, grasping and pinching. Ilse let out a screamed obscenity. The pestilence that had fastened onto

Michelle's bag backed off. The people, clothed like crow's feathers over sticks, climbed over one another, their eyes red, their haunted faces like those of drug addicts, as they thirsted after food.

Weakly Michelle stayed put. With her last vestige of strength Ilse grabbed hard at a neck. She shook it until it spoke. The person, if it was a person – it behaved more like a locust – anyway, it obeyed her command to speak. In between parched demands for water, it told her they were at Heimstadt.

'Hitler is dead,' said a voice from the platform. When Ilse located the man who had spoken, he also was dead. He leaned against others who had gone before him. They were the remnants from previous train-loads who had been lured here by rumours of plenty. In no time at all the wagon was denuded of everything. All that remained were Michelle and Ilse lying in the corner. Michelle managed a feeble joke.

'We're unclaimed treasure. They don't know what they missed,' she murmured, her eyes focussing enough to take in the scenes of hell that stretched in all directions.

'I think we've seen it all before,' said Ilse. Then she saw Hans. His mouth hung open, his eyes were saucer-shaped with horror. The old hackneyed phrase swam through her mind: out of the frying-pan and into the fire. There were no forests for hunting in; the only thing in ready supply at Heimstadt was people.

As a young women Red Cross worker picked her way amongst the heaps that cried for water, their three men companions sat dazed on the floor of the wagon, a picture of defeated German manhood. They were amongst millions whose pilot-light of survival was burning dangerously low. The war was over. Where were the flags? The carnival? The joy? The relief? No guards prodded them with guns. No official asked to see their papers.

Ilse couldn't look. She had never got used to it. People who had once had homes, jobs, families, all the things that give structure and purpose, were queuing, crying, sleeping, dying – some quietly, some noisily resisting all the way. An adult woman was clutching tightly to her teddy bear. It had a pale blue ribbon around its neck. And the stench. . . .

Under roof architecture demented by war, the five drew breath. Did any of them have a clue as to what next?

Ernst's filth-marked head lifted creakily on its scrawny neck. As he looked at each of them in turn he seemed to be weighing something over. At last he said, 'Ilse.' As he spoke her name, he jerked his head towards some wobbly letters painted in red on a mobile unit. The words could not have read more beautifully than Goethe's finest writings: RED CROSS.

Ilse gave an ironic grunt. There were always two threads weaving their way through the cloth of her life: Red Cross and trains.

Ernst and Ilse left the others. 'Come on,' he said, 'I need help carrying the soup.'

A sob rose half-way up her throat. The last time she had tasted soup was at the farm. In months it was not long ago. In experience it was a hundred kilometres beyond the closed doors of her youth. So many of her generation were dead or on the way there.

They joined the mamouth queue. 'Waitress service,' said Ilse grimly, as she watched helpers from the Auxillary War Service bring soup to those who could not get up to fetch for themselves.

When they returned to their bivouac, the wagons had gone. A pillow had been formed from Hans' coat, and all three lay stretched out like a row of fish drying on a beach. They were the lucky ones. Sleep had rescued them from reality for a short while.

'Leave 'em be,' said Ernst.

Without any shame at what they did, they scoffed all the soup. I'll get some more when they wake, Ilse reassured herself. She checked her boot heels, then lay down to rest.

In her sleep, hunger savaged her stomach like wild dogs at their kill. The wind howled. A gaunt white figure in monk-like habit and faceless hood said. *'Der Wind, der Wind, der himmlische Wind.'* ('The wind, the wind, the heavenly wind.') A finger the length of a python tapped her shoulder.

She woke to find Ernst shaking her shoulder.

'Ilse, Ilse, come on. We must find food before they wake.'

'I can't,' she said. 'Just leave me here.'

'Come on. You must. We're the youngest.'

Groggily she unfolded herself limb by painful limb until she was standing beside him, towering almost half a head taller than he. For all his lack of height, though, Ernst had become huge in stature to them.

Somehow she became separated from him. A recently-arrived train disgorged men with hands pummelled to calluses by gruelling labour, probably in some mine deep in Russia's communist heart. They had bodies from which the last ounce of graft had been wrung, and clothes marked with the colour of the terrain's soil. Silently they jostled, and Ilse was sucked into their midst as they surged towards a hoped-for Shangri-La.

The mob milled through the broken hole in the wall that acted as a door. These searchers after the promised land, visibly marked by adversity, moaned as one voice when they saw what was before them. A drizzle filled in the time between daylight and darkness, adding threateningly to the unfamiliarity of the city. It fell comfortless upon kilometres of rubble, some only shoulder-high. A few warehouses hugged the station wall. Where was the warmth, merriment and swinging coloured lights of that far-off Christmas when Mutti and Vati had taken her to the children's show? The stores had been piled with goodies, and shoppers made their choices to the sound of *Stille Nache* and *O Tannenbaum*. It was certainly *Stille Nacht* now.

Disappointment turned to anger, then to violence. A man with an iron bar attacked the warehouse door as if it were his enemy. Sounds of rage grew in their throats as people followed him into the darkness. Ilse was carried along. No one took any notice of her. Nothing worth stealing on her personage, and she looked just like a chap. The blonde tresses were gone. Michelle had cut them off when they both got lice. They'd searched out fennel and rubbed it in, binding their heads with huge leaves, and at last they'd flushed out the little devils.

In the gloom, promising cardboard boxes and plywood chests were visible. Like too many rats finding too little food, they swarmed over them, gashing and clawing to reveal bottles and magnums of wine and spirits, cigarettes and clothes. Cigarettes! It was far better than finding banknotes. They had become the currency of the day. They could buy wonderful things like potatoes, poultry, bacon, eggs and flour. At the very worst, they could be smoked to quell the pangs of hunger.

Along with the others, Ilse fought dirty with elbows and feet. She squealed in agony as someone latched onto her newly growing hair. She pulled away. Still they persisted, willing her to give way on her position near the cigarettes. She would not. No way. The sacrifice was some of her hair and skin. As fast as she filled Karl's long-pocketed gift trousers, then it seemed thousands of hands attempted to unfill them. Her adrenalin was running high on the lawlessness. Not since the long-jump final against her disliked rival at school had she felt this charged up.

Shots spat out. The looters shrank back.

'Get out of here – NOW. We're in charge, a British voice commanded.

Ilse couldn't believe it, but they obeyed the voice. The aggressive rats became mice that crept out into the night. Before the game was up, Ilse had managed to purloin a good share of the booty.

As if she were a veteran shop-lifter or Christmas sales expert, she had shrugged on a coat of the most appalling lime green hue whilst seeing off the cigarette grabbers.

The gunshots had created instant order out of chaos. The ragged human beings from the bottom of the status pile trooped like a convent school crocodile out of the warehouse. The miners, her criminal collaborators of the previous moment, must have melted into a hole. Where did they all go? How would they eat? They weren't even a number on a list. Just gone into the night. No sinking into the pillowy bosom of a warm home for them. Instead there lay ahead of them the ruins of a city that would offer them rejection.

She could have been back in Liga on the morning after the bombs, except for the street being utterly deserted. It was more frightening than the enraged mob with whom she had surged between the skeleton buildings. Now whilst scurrying, she took off the new coat and her original overcoat that had been through too many hedges and ditches. She put the old one over her new one and again became part of the drab landscape. They probably shot looters. Now the war was over no one would look twice at a refugee.

'Where the hell have you been?' demanded Michelle angrily. Her face was ugly with worry and her deloused short hair stood up in spikes. She was locking and unlocking her fingers. Proudly Ilse undid her old coat to reveal the startling newness of the one underneath.

'Doesn't suit you,' said Michelle, trying hard to conceal her curiosity.

'It's for our interviews and it would suit you,' came Ilse's fast reply.

'Interviews! Now you really have gone crazy. I haven't the strength to crack an egg open, even if one exists within twenty kilometres of here.'

'I can supply those too. Look.' Before showing her cigarette haul she glanced around furtively. Everyone was too preoccupied with their own suffering.

Michelle's eyes widened in amazement. 'Whew,' she whistled.

Hans, who had kept out of the slight bickering that was going on between the two women, leaned forward for a better look.

'Treasure trove. How do you do it? You've an uncanny knack of being in the right place at the crucial moment.'

'Forgiven?' Ilse winked at Michelle.

'I was worried. By the way, what are you doing?'

Ilse was examining Michelle's feet. 'Just seeing what size feet you've got,' she said mysteriously.

'You should know that by now.'

'Got a spot of business to do.' Ilse wandered off, picking her way through the human carpet.

'Wonder what she'll do when we get sorted out,'

mused Karl as he watched her scrutinizing people's feet. At last she bent down by a woman whose head and shoulders were covered by a shawl. It was difficult to tell her age. In these times you grew old with dramatic suddenness. As Ilse talked to her she put her head to one side in a listening pose. At last there was a nod. Shoes were swapped. Before putting Ilse's on her feet, the shawl woman checked inside the shoe by pulling up the lining. She seemed well pleased.

'Size six shoes in excellent condition,' smiled Ilse at the four upturned questioning faces. 'An investment in our careers. One coat, a pair of shoes and the British in authority could mean a job interview. We all speak English, don't we? Some of us'll have to find work.'

'And she gave you those shoes for your pongy old water-shippers?' Michelle was still fascinated by Ilse's bartering skills.

'Mutti gave me a gold bracelet for exchanging for food. It's been in the heel of my boot ever since I left home. I can use the coat and shoes for an interview, then you can use them. Like I said, career progression.'

'I don't reckon green's my colour,' said Ernst, straightfaced. It was his first stab at humour since they'd met him.

'Oh, I think you'd look rather pretty. You may be just what the interviewing officer's looking for,' said Michelle mischievously.

They stayed near the soup and rested for long periods of time, willing their bodies to gather strength. Work and a roof over their heads were the all-important goals. The chances were slim, the competition fierce.

The gold bracelet, which had been in the Weinacht family for three generations, passed down from Czech ancestors, entered the global bartering system. The going rate – one pair of second-hand shoes.

BOOK II

16

Squadron Leader Freddie Wheeler stood cross-armed at the window of his newly acquired office. A cigarette was at his lips, and the lines around his eyes crinkled musingly. Jolly decent view; the whole of the parade-ground could be seen. He liked that. Top-hole. It formed the kernel of the camp from which a galaxy of doorways led to a hubbub of administrative offices. Round the bend of each corridor the doors seemed to breed. From behind their thin cheap wood came the buzz of activity.

The Squadron Leader shared his room with a large double-fronted oak desk on which were heaped buff files bearing fascinating titles like 'RAF. Heimstadt – Loo Rolls'. With statistics like nine hundred overcoats per four hundred thousand people, Freddie Wheeler, Equipment Officer, was a useful chap to know. It was his first morning at the recently assembled RAF camp. Staff recruitment day had spawned a deal of activity that toed and froed across the parade square. Human life spanning the entire spectrum of physical and sartorial disrepair came and went. Held together by hope, they began as black dots at the entrance to the distant airfield, growing larger as they entered the quadrangle, then disappearing into the double yellow swing doors beneath his office.

A coat of the most God-awful green joined the trickle

of people. As it got nearer he could see it was far too big for the – yes, it was a woman – skinny person inside. Lovely legs. The coat was short enough to reveal a fair expanse of thin well-shaped unstockinged legs which ended in athletic ankles and sensible walking shoes. The wind lifted the short jagged ends of dark-blonde hair. Couldn't be young. Walked too slowly.

'Thoroughbred,' murmured the experienced Freddie. He didn't know who the hell she was but there was a sense of bereavement when the yellow doors claimed her.

Inside the building, Ilse's nose twitched at the smell of fresh paint, a new and exciting bouquet. The décor was subdued magnolia. Cloakroom? Where was it? She must at all costs get there before the interview. Their bed-sit under the departure board – non-operational, of course – did not as yet have the benefit of running water. There it was. 'Ladies'. The room was empty. It had fitted carpet and soap! Real soap! It was a large white block. Cheap. Odourless. Soap! Soap! She held it tightly to check it was no mirage. Swiftly opening her coat, she washed beneath the sleeveless woollen vest and rolled-up men's trousers Karl had got for them. These two articles of clothing comprised her underwear.

Decorously the door opened.

'Morning,' said a WRAF officer in a much decorated uniform. The short, black-haired woman disappeared into one of the cubicles. When she came out to wash her hands, there was an expression of total unconcern on her face. It was as if finding a strangely dressed woman washing her feet in a basin in the ladies' loo was a daily occurrence. The slim, sophisticated officer dried her hands on a towel. It was then that Ilse caught the sidelong glance of amusement in the mirror. The important person went out, leaving behind the fragrance of someone who has recently had a bath. Were all the British so nonchalant? Fancy not being stopped, questioned, reprimanded, punished. It was this new freedom that gave her a spurt of joy as she stepped out into the corridor and took her place in the long interview queue.

Ilse watched as Miss Efficiency 1945 dealt with a gaggle of hopefuls at the counter. Wouldn't like her as a boss. Miss Birgit Fortesque gave dismissive glances over half-moon spectacles at those of obviously inferior status. The look varied according to the employability of the person. Barely restrained by her uniform tunic, her overlarge non-calorie-controlled bust heaved with the importance of it all. She was here to help these poor people.

Having been awake since first light, unsurprisingly Ilse nodded off. Birgit became an eagle, her talons grabbing those she selected to work for her. There was a printed notice on the counter declaring Birgit's name and job description: 'Miss Birgit Fortesque – Personnel Officer'.

Ilse awoke to a finger prod.

'You're next,' said the woman next to her. All the job applicants seemed to be female.

The space between the metal-framed chair with its bit of cloth for a seat and the counter seemed a long way. As she circumnavigated this vast distance she felt Birgit's eyes sizing up her finger-combed hair, cheap coat, bare legs and over-large boot-style shoes.

Like a barrage from a machine-gun Birgit fired questions.

'Name?'
'Nationality?'
'Date of Birth?'

'Qualifications?'

At the answer 'German', Birgit's lips pursed, but when Ilse replied in accentless English that her qualifications were English language, typing, shorthand in English and German and general office skills, there were signs of approval as Miss Fortesque looked up and removed her intimidating glasses.

'Do you have papers?' she asked, as if she was tired of the question and well knew the answer.

'Lost in the bombing.' Not strictly true but it seemed easier than trying to explain she'd spent the past few months in a forest dodging Russians.

'Last post held?'

'Auxiliary nurse, Red Cross, Liga Central Station.'

Birgit Fortesque's face stayed immobile for quite a time. The muscles readied themselves for the next question but then changed their minds.

'Thank you,' she said quietly, almost with respect. 'I'll see if Squadron Leader Wheeler is free. Please wait here.'

When Birgit had gone, Ilse's chin sunk to her chest. The rats were at it again, gnawing away in her stomach. Soup was not keeping them quiet. She must get this job or she and they were dead. She did not see Birgit glance back. Before slipping through into the chief's office she turned round and looked thoughtfully at Fräulein Weinacht's slumped head.

Wheeler looked up irritably from his desk.

'Oh hello, Superwoman,' he said. 'Thought it was someone I didn't want to see. Problems?'

'On the contrary, sir. Young woman, speaks fluent English. Could be suitable for the post of secretary.'

He doodled on the leather-cornered blotter. 'How soon can she start? We've a helluva lot of orders to meet and the chaps on these construction sites don't speak English.'

'I'd guess she'd be only too desperate to start straight away. I'm sure she's been living rough, although she's done a pretty good job at sprucing herself up. She's from Liga.'

'Liga! Good God, give her the job. I want excellent English and gorgeous legs. Give her a ration card for the canteen before she goes.'

Birgit's face boggled. 'Yes, sir.'

Wheeler pulled open the top desk drawer. A strong smell of snuff and peppermints filled the room. He fought to close the drawer. It didn't run smoothly at all. As he sucked a mint he smirked wickedly at Birgit's complete inability to know when her tubby leg was being pulled.

She mustn't collapse here. Please God, not here. They'd think she wasn't up to the job. Her head felt as though it would drop off. Each time her chin neared her chest she jerked herself upright. She saw Miss Fortesque come back into the hall. Her head sunk again. She noticed how the woman's feet splayed out as she walked. What was it Mutti always said? 'You have to fight every day or you go under.' She had certainly found that out.

'Squadron Leader Wheeler will see you, Miss Weinacht.' Birgit was going to say "now", but even she was capable of occasionally giving someone a break.

'I'll arrange the interview for after lunch. I have instructions to give you this.' She pressed a coupon into Ilse's hand.

'Thank you. Thank you.' Ilse turned it over and over in her hand in disbelief. Then she remembered why she was here.

'What time would you like me here?' she stammered, still overcome by this bounty. She'd been in a world which for years had offered no free meals.

'Two o'clock would be fine.'

'Two o'clock,' repeated Ilse. 'If you don't mind I'll just sit here for a while. I've got a touch of cramp.'

'As you wish, Miss Weinacht.'

Ilse waited until Birgit was busy before she risked making a move to find the staff canteen. Could she get out of the hall without making an exhibition of herself and fainting? She lurched a few steps at a time. They'd thing she was drunk. She wished she was.

Birgit's beady eyes didn't miss anything. She saw Miss Weinacht grab a door-handle and escape into the corridor.

'Name,' she demanded of the next set of desperate eyes.

It was a large, many-windowed room, and oddly, unlike the luxury accorded to the ladies' loo, without the benefit of fitted carpets. Instead, between the door and the paper-laden desk, an oriental prayer-mat adorned the floor. A shortish man, his back to her, was gazing out of the window. Funny how you got used to noticing whether someone looked strong or not. Being capable of work was a valuable asset during and after war. If the hard labour didn't kill you off, it kept you alive. You were too useful to be shot or starved.

At the sound of the door-handle's jerk, the meditating man turned to face her. He had a charming smile. She felt his scarcely suppressed energy. With a nicotined finger he stabbed at a sheet of paper, then he came towards her. How could men like him have bombed Liga?

'Allow me to take your coat, Fräulein Weinacht.'

'Thank you, uh, no thank you. I think I'll keep it on. I've had a bit of a chill.' She was sweating with nerves. He spoke gently in perfect German but considering the

paucity of the garments under her coat he might just as well have said, 'Would you like to be shot?'
'Please take a seat. I won't keep you a moment.'
'Thank you.' How grateful she was to sit down. He would surely notice her trembling. Not even a handbag to clutch tightly. There was silence whilst he studied some notes. His bristly moustache and slicked-back hair were light brown. There was not a trace of balding. He could be late thirties or early forties. He wore no ring, but then she'd heard British men didn't. Using a gold-topped maroon fountain pen he scribbled something on a pad. He had such clean finger-nails. Instinctively she curled her own underneath the palms of her hands. There were some places soap would not reach. *Please God let him give me the job.* It meant everything. How subordinate she felt. He had the power to place a roof over her head or consign her to scavenging like an animal off the streets, living off other people's rubbish. Did he know that? He looked up. 'Fräulein Weinacht, I see you speak fluent English and are qualified in typing and shorthand.'
'Yes, sir.'
'How is that?'
'I studied English at school, after which I worked for an export firm that dealt with Britain. At the same time I attended night-school, where I obtained certificates in English shorthand.'
'It's obviously something that's going to be most useful at this time. We're involved in ordering supplies from Britain and distributing them in this part of Germany. There would be a fair amount of technical translation involving machine components, and' – he laughed, then waved towards the burgeoning file on his desk-top – 'mammoth distribution of loo paper.'
Ilse laughed with him. Oh, it felt good. His buoyancy

was infectious. Nothing of the energy-sapper about him. Surely he must inject those around him with vitality. It was almost as if during this serious attempt at an interview he was struggling to keep his sense of humour under wraps.

'Are you presently in employment? I mean, would we have to wait until you'd worked out your notice?'

He'd got to be joking. Was it his way of paying her respect? Wasn't it blatantly obvious she was a member of the unwashed and dispossessed?

'No, I'm not in a job at present.'

'And your previous job, Fräulein Weinacht?'

'Nursing auxiliary with the Red Cross.'

His hands were laid palms downwards on the desk. He looked past her to a spot on the prayer-mat. His bottom teeth nicked his top lip.

'Liga, I gather.'

She nodded.

'Would you be interested in the post as secretary? You'd be working for me but directly responsible to Miss Fortesque.'

'I'd like to work here very much, sir.' She tried to sound as though he hadn't offered her the world. Even the ghastly Birgit would seem like an angel at the gates of heaven.

'Mind you, it wouldn't be for a couple of weeks. We need you now, but we've no typewriters. Perhaps you could let Miss Fortesque know your whereabouts so that we can let you know a starting date?'

'Um, I'm a bit mobile just at the moment. Perhaps I could arrange a date to call in?'

He didn't say any more, so she got to her feet.

'Thank you, Squadron Leader Wheeler, for seeing me. I'll do my very best.'

'I'm sure you will.' He darted over to open the door.

Out in the corridor she leaned against the wall. Her heart was racing.

'Thank you, English shorthand. You got me off the streets.' Her head was upturned to the ceiling.

Wheeler drew on a cigarette. He watched the green coat out of sight.

'Wonderful ankles,' he sighed and reached for the file on earth-moving equipment.

17

'The return of the bread-winner, we hope. Any luck, old thing?' Michelle looked up expectantly from her place on the coats on the station platform.

Ilse's grin spread from earlobe to earlobe, followed by a victorious thumbs-up sign.

'You bet. Start in about two weeks. Got to check in sometime to find out a definite date.'

'Oh, you genius,' yelled Michelle, pumping her arm.

'You'd better be nice to me if you want me for my money,' quipped Ilse, sticking her nose haughtily in the air.

'You're not kidding. I knew when I was onto a good thing.'

'We are unmanned.' Hans spread his arms out in a dramatic gesture.

'Stupid, that'll be the day! So what happened with you?' Ilse cuffed him playfully around the head.

'We're all right too,' said Karl, his damaged face muscles twitching, so they knew he was smiling. 'On the bridge-building site. Not brain-challenging, lousy rations and no hostel accommodation until we've built it,' he ended ruefully.

'When you snaffled that coat, pretty remiss of you not to bring the champagne as well. Oh well, it'll have to be a soup party tonight. By the way, love, may I borrow your coat and shoes tomorrow? The news is getting worse. Armageddon just outside pretty little villages. Looks like I'll be needed.' Michelle slumped back a little tiredly, as if the air had gone out of a bicycle tyre.

'You don't have to go, you know. As long as one of us has something,' said Ilse, doubting whether Michelle had sufficient strength left to back up her unceasing need to be of some use.

'I'll be OK. Don't worry.' There was little further chat, but a new ingredient had been added to their pinched faces – hope.

'Where exactly is it that you're going?' said Ilse, breathless from the walk. They were on the move again, this time in search of accommodation. It meant a visit to a Freemason colleague of Vati's to investigate whether his house still stood. The *Trümmerfrauen* were out in force – hundreds of rubble women picking up bricks that could be reused and piling them onto huge mounds out of which grass was already growing.

'They didn't say exactly. They need anyone with the slightest sniff of medical knowledge. Talk is that there are about forty thousand people in the most terrible state. They're scared witless about a typhus outbreak. I'm to be at the station at seven in the morning on Friday.'

Ilse took her arm. It wasn't the same Michelle who had come out of Liga with her. She stumbled a lot, seeming unsure where before she had been such a positive force.

'Here we are, Luftstrasse.'

They looked up at a three storey family house that was now probably split into flats. Gardens spread from all sides. Between the garden and the street were railings and a thick, neglected hedge. Amongst weeds, flowers nodded along each side of the broken crazy-paved path that led to the front door. Set in the wall was a brass plate with the words: *W. Tannenbaun. Dental Surgeon.*

Ilse checked Michelle by placing a hand on her shoulder. 'We're in luck.'

Michelle looked doubtfully down at her clothes and footwear. 'You go. They'll have a fit if they see me.'

'Wait here then.' Ilse shoved the rucksack into her friend's hands, strode purposefully up to the door and pounded the brass knocker. It reminded her of her first childhood home. The haunts of her early youth now no longer existed, and it was as though part of herself had been erased. There was no longer any geographical proof that she was ever young. A holy place had been desecrated.

There was movement behind the stained glass. In the door opening stood a middle-aged woman with dark braided hair.

'Frau Tannenbaum?'

'Who are you?' said the woman, reluctant to talk to strangers.

'Ilse Weinacht. My father and Herr Tannenbaum belonged to the same lodge in Liga.'

'Liga. My daughter lived in Liga.' The woman's face changed terribly and she made as if to close the door.

'Who is it, dear?' asked a voice from the recess off the hall.

'No one. No one at all.'

'I thought there were no more patients today?'

'A beggar.' She looked at Ilse's dirty finger-nails and boots with contempt. The door began to close.

'Please,' pleaded Ilse. A tall, thin man with a shock of white hair and deep lines down the centre of each cheek walked down the hall. He was polishing a pair of spectacles like Vati's. Ilse's heart was breaking. The door banged in her face. She sank onto the doorstep. Her mother's words came back. *The world revolves round love and money.* She had nothing so she was nothing. There were furious whisperings behind the door. When she was half-way down the path it opened again.

'My wife tells me you're Weinacht's daughter.'

'Yes,' said Ilse to the man, who looked worried to death. 'I believe my father knew you when you practised in Liga.'

'Forgive us. The British army have taken over our house. All except the work-room. We thought you were more trouble.' He looked so old and sad.

'I'm looking for a room. I have a job – I can pay. I'd only be in for a few hours at night. Can you help me? Please.'

'I wish I could help but we have no room. We go along the road to share with my brother when we finish work.'

Ilse nodded dejectedly and turned to leave.

'Don't go. At least let us give you something to eat.'

'May I call my friend?'

'Please.'

'Michelle, Michelle,' she shouted, and went quickly down the path to see where her friend was. She was sitting on the grass verge, her head resting in her hands. At the call, she heaved herself slowly up and walked down the path to join them.

Herr Tannenbaum could not hide his look of pity. This girl was worse than the other one. He ushered them in, seating them in the tiny waiting-room which held three red canvas-seated chairs and a coffee table on which was a non-political magazine. They were left alone.

Michelle made a grimace as if to say, 'What's going to

happen now, I wonder?' Ilse felt an overwhelming rush of love and fear. She couldn't think of life without Michelle and yet if she went to that camp. . . . Suddenly she examined her hands, not wanting her friend to see the look on her face.

'My wife and I have been thinking. We could offer you this waiting-room as temporary shelter until you find something. Obviously you wouldn't be able to use it during the day,' said Herr Tannenbaum, handing them coffee and unbuttered black bread. Ilse checked to see if he was serious. They were being offered a palace. There was disbelief on Michelle's face.

'Thank you, I can't tell you how grateful we are. I don't start my job though for two weeks,' said Ilse doubtfully.

'Members of a lodge are obliged to help their friends and their friends' children. It's not a favour. You pay when you start your job.'

Ilse pumped his hand repeatedly up and down.

Herr Tannenbaum stood at the door watching them leave. The older woman was severely weakened. She was steadied by the younger one, who gave her a quick hug and a peck on the cheek. Because of the hedge they were soon out of sight.

'War,' he said wearily, 'when will we ever learn?'

It was their last night. The men had gone to their bridge-building project. Ilse had yet to begin her job at the British RAF base, but Michelle was leaving in the morning, bound with a team of other medics for a recently liberated camp where it had been confirmed virulent disease had broken out. They had moved into the dentist's waiting area.

A single-bar electric fire lit the room, its red slivers

glowing up the white-painted walls. They sat close to its heat, although it was not a chilly night. A strange tension filled the silence. Regularly Michelle bobbed up to check her medical bag. She seemed to crave being occupied, and her face had a shut-in look.

'What *is* the matter? You're like a flea,' said Ilse at last in irritation. 'It's our last night. You might at least talk to me.'

There was no response from Michelle. Instead she turned away, wrapping her arms around herself as if cold. Her shoulder-blades protruded in points through the print dress borrowed from Frau Tannenbaum, and she shook a little.

'Is it what we've heard about the camps?' asked Ilse, moving closer.

Michelle shook her head.

'Hey, come on,' said Ilse. Gently as a butterfly settling, she touched her shoulder. The wretchedness in Michelle's eyes was unbearable.

'Come here.' Ilse held her friend close and sighed. Tomorrow. Damn tomorrow. They couldn't exactly pop on a train or back a car out of a suburban garage and nip to the next town to take tea with each other. It was the desolation of departure. The feeling when swallows line up on telephone lines and mooring ropes and you know they are leaving you. They are travelling thousands of kilometres and you won't see them until next year – if they make it. A prelude to the icy crawl through interminable winter nights.

'You've an early start in the morning.'

'I know,' said Michelle.

18

The night terrors began the day Michelle left. The same scenario, its power never waned. Rarely again did she know the kind of sleep that took away the cares of the day.

A goods train painted in dark rust drew into a station. Though old and in the last stages of disrepair, it made not a sound. The carriages were of the closed variety; the type used for transporting cattle. Narrow slits allowed in air and a modicum of light. These gouges along the middle of each truck seemed like half-shut eyes not daring to open fully in case the outside world might know its secrets. Human arms dangled from the apertures. Occasionally one of them waved, but most just hung loose. Everything was covered in cobwebs of despair. It was always dark. Gusts howled through the night-time. Eventually the train would stop at an isolated station.

It was at this stage that Ilse left the train, which then disappeared into a black hole. After passing through an empty waiting-room, she turned left out of the door. She knew that each step took her closer to something horrible, but her legs would not turn round. Whatever it was was so obscene that the dream in its mercy never revealed it to her. There was one clue. Carrying on the wind, wailing human voices.

Watching Michelle board the train was hell. You never know when you do something for the last time or see a person for the last time. Like blood flowing from a severed artery, she almost felt strength draining from her.

Michelle turned and waved before disappearing into the body of the train. It would be the usual bun-fight to find some space to stand, let alone sit. Anxiously Ilse watched from the platform, hoping she would re-appear. She must have got hemmed in away from a window. Ilse waved the train out of sight and beyond. She stayed on the same spot for a long time, looking at the space where the train had been. All gone now. All her loved ones were somewhere else.

'Hey, lady, you growing there or summat?' said an official. They moved her on as if she was a tramp cluttering up a park bench.

Surely the week that followed must have lasted for a year? In comparison, fire-storms and street fighting seemed inconveniences. She had never experienced loneliness of such intensity, to walk along the road of a strange town and know there was no likelihood she'd meet anyone she knew. All the gang had dispersed. They went like seeds from a sycamore, once so bonded, but going when it was time, and never again returning to the mother tree.

Her bedroom went back to its original function of dentist's waiting-room during business hours. Frau Tannenbaum allowed her half an hour's use of her brother-in-law's kitchen along the road in the evening so that she could warm the Aid for Refugees' watery soup with its minuscule piece of meat in it – if you got lucky that day. The job was the Holy Grail, but as the days dragged it seemed to hover elusively on the distant horizon.

During that week Ilse could often be found sitting at Heimstadt Station amongst the eastbound hordes of home-goers; a tiny proportion of the displaced persons, thirteen million of whom were going home. The platform groaned under the weight of so many feet; forced labourers, concentration camp survivors, prisoners of war – you name it, they were there. 'Going home', now there's a phrase, Ilse thought. How she wished she was 'going home'. But how could she? Her parents were now in the Soviet zone, and against all the odds she now had a job. She must be good at it and keep it.

She found out that there are varieties of loneliness. It wasn't people she needed, but those of her own tribe, those who knew her, who wordlessly understood, who were deeply embroidered into the fabric of her life. She realized now the insidious effects of loneliness and how it could lead to illness. She would never again find ease in getting to know people or allow herself the luxury of depending on anyone but herself. However settled she might appear to the outer world, emotionally she would always be ready for flight.

Ilse's was the type of face people trusted and felt inclined to unburden their troubles to. Thus she learned she was one of the lucky ones. A room, a job, soup at the station. What more could one possibly expect from life? And yet, oh, to talk with the one that lifted the spirit; that gave reason to being and fighting.

Doing nothing is a pleasure when the weather is sunny and you've money in your pocket. Though summer, it rained miserably day after dreary day. She had no money even for postage stamps, not that the Germans were allowed to mail letters, anyway. She wrote on some wrapping-paper found in a street, then begged someone with a kind face bound for Liga to deliver it to Herr Weinacht. In the note she asked Vati to try to get word via Herr Tannenbaum.

All things end. Unbelievably, that week did and she began her new life.

Her first day at the office. The Russian army and clandestine train journeys paled against this. It mattered too much. This was her one chance to move up in the world. She'd better be good, damn good. In her borrowed floral dress and green coat she crossed the parade ground at a sharper pace than on her previous visits. Though isolated and still on a meagre diet, she had had the opportunity to rest. The burden of being a fugitive had been lifted. Before entering the swing doors she glanced up at the boss's office. No one was there. Warily she entered the zone where she had done her marathon queuing.

Efficiency's most ardent disciple, Birgit, couldn't help a look at her watch as Ilse entered the hall. Her tight mouth relaxed into a smile of approval at the punctuality.

'Good morning,' she said. Without waiting for a reply she ushered her new charge into a sunlit office containing three desks and two typewriters.

'I sit here.' She waved towards the typewriterless desk under the window overlooking the parade-ground.

'Renate will be in this morning. Choose either of the other two.' She smiled like a friendly cobra.

'Thank you,' said Ilse, taking off her coat and putting her bottle of flour and water on the desk under the notice-board.

'You'll need these to start with.' Birgit handed her two small volumes of instructions. 'Perhaps you'd like to look at them whilst I sort out some work?'

Left alone, Ilse decided she must be in heaven. A cushioned chair was not a comfort to be underestimated when you had little in the way of padding around the rear end. Since leaving her parents' home the only seating on offer had been the waiting room chairs at the digs and a railway bench – when vacant – at Heimstadt Station.

The first handbook was an operator's manual for maintaining the RAF's mechanical appliances and motor vehicles. She was not in the least mechanically minded, and the technical words were as unfamiliar to her in German as they were in English. She sweated at the thought of having to take these words down in shorthand and vowed to get hold of a shorthand dictionary so she could add to her limited vocabulary.

The other book was a more personal document. It decreed no fraternization between the Germans and the British. The only interaction allowed was to be in the work-place. The conquered nation was not permitted to socialize with the conquerors. Separate cubicles at hairdressers, different queues for the cinema, forbidden restaurants, etc., etc. Suits me, she shrugged, so long as they pay my rent. I'll leave politics to others. Food in the belly was her priority. For the first time the cards in her hand were good. She was going to play them with the utmost care. If she didn't, she could stay at the bottom of the heap.

The door opened and a woman of about forty entered. Superb dress sense, Ilse judged by her freshly laundered white blouse and black skirt. Her blonde hair was greying at the temples, and her eyes were the blue of a song-thrush's egg. Her nose was straight – not like my ski-jump of a nose, envied Ilse. She looked worried but then broke into a smile on seeing Ilse.

'Hello, I'm Renate. Pleased to meet you. First day

too?' said Ilse's office colleague, coming forward to shake hands. 'Well, I say first day, but I did a couple of days last week. Sudden delivery of equipment and they needed someone to process the paperwork. As you can see, I'm an old hand. Anything I can help you with from my two days' experience, just let me know.' Renate hung up the coat she had carried over her arm. Its black colour almost disguised the burn marks. You too, thought Ilse.

'I've been reading these books from Miss Fortesque.'

'Oh, those,' said Renate dismissively. 'Most of the officers we work for speak some German; and the frat regulations, well, I think you'll find human nature will bypass those.' Renate laughed airily. Ilse felt at ease immediately. The loneliness must have happened to someone else. Here was an ally to stand with her on the Anti-Birgit Committee.

'Busybodying somewhere?' asked Renate, nodding towards the Personal Assistant of the Year's empty desk.

'Probably,' giggled Ilse. It felt as if it was the first day at junior school and they were sorting out lockers and which peg for their shoebags.

Renate took in Ilse's stick arms and slow movement.

'Here.' She produced a packet of sandwiches from her stained canvas laundry bag. She divided them fairly into two. Renate laughed as Ilse's eyes grew wide with questions, her mouth dropping open in amazement that anyone she knew should own such a parcel of luxury let alone share it with her.

'Don't let Her see them. I don't want to be interrogated as to my source of supply.' Renate's head inclined towards the door that led to the outer office, where no doubt even as they ate, Birgit was dispensing her good works.

'Mother works in the canteen. There's plenty of spares at the end of the day. Hence my blossoming figure.' She rolled up her sleeve and put her plumpish arm next to Ilse's. 'You too can look like me if you eat left-overs.' They giggled conspiratorially. With an eye on the dangerous door, Ilse wolfed down the bread and cheese. Even through the nausea as her stomach rebelled against the unaccustomed overtime, Ilse breathed a sigh of ecstasy.

Renate rattled away on her typewriter at impressive speed, while Ilse turned the pages of her unriveting technical handbooks slowly. It was peaceful. No screams. No gunshots. No one jumping out of bushes. And *food*.

The door whammed against the jamb with such force it had got to be lying in splinters? Before disappearing into his office, Whirlwind Wheeler bawled 'Morning' at his staff.

With the second door he made a din equal to the first. Birgit, who had by now rejoined her minions, looked longingly at the sealed portal whence her master had gone. Renate winked at Ilse. Birgit saw it and looked annoyed. Then all three bent their heads over their work.

Later, as they queued for the canteen, Ilse asked, 'What was all that about?'

'Oh you know, office gossip,' replied Renate tantalizingly.

'You can't leave me in the air like that.'

'And I thought at last I'd met a woman of integrity. A human being who lives above office gossip.'

'Oh come on, give.'

Renate drew an enormous breath. Her expression said, 'I have a matter of deepest international significance to impart to you.' Ilse followed suit with an equally serious face.

'Funny thing, it's always Friday when the Big White Chief rams the door down. My sources reveal – actually it's the girl in the post-room – that his letters from America usually arrive on a Friday. Reggie – Oh Good old Reggie, you'll meet him soon enough – who was transferred here along with Wheeler, says he's got a woman over there. Trouble is she's got a husband. Looks like he's got it bad, huh?'

'Mmm,' replied Ilse, presenting her ration card, which got her a serving spoonful of stew, some gravy which was more water than anything else and two bullets of potatoes. She felt gratitude. This was all for her. Ilse's concentration had left Renate's chatter.

'Birgit, as you may have noticed, has the hots for her boss, who can't get his mind off his American piece. Meanwhile Reggie fancies Birgit, who doesn't reciprocate, and I'm hoping my man will come back from the front. Or am I?' finished Renate, a little out of breath. Her last bit of information got back Ilse's attention.

'I'm so sorry.'

'Don't be. If he did come back he'd probably be in such a state that I wouldn't be able to cope. A lot of them are, you know. I've got used to independence. Oh and I forgot to say, no one's fancying me because they know I've got no money and no home. My English got me a box-room on the camp.'

'You won't be on your own for long,' said Ilse.

'That'll get you a long way,' replied her first day's mentor appreciatively.

'What will?' said Ilse, trying not to eat quickly but not being able to help herself behaving like a pig at a trough.

'Charm,' smiled Renate wisely. 'You've got it.'

'Oh dear,' said Ilse.

'What do you mean "Oh dear"? Use it. Don't hide your light under a bush,' advised the worldly Renate.

The afternoon was spent typing up lists. Unaccustomed to food in the middle of the day, Ilse felt heavy-lidded, desperately wanting to sleep. List upon list of mechanical diggers and vehicles destined for outlying villages. What on earth for? Industry was in ruins and she'd heard they weren't allowing Germans to start any new businesses. One of the villages bore the name Michelle had mentioned. Was she there? The Germans were still not allowed to send or receive letters, but sometimes a message got through via a human chain. Ilse had received no such message. Her isolation was total. All she could try was telepathy.

Ilse's first duty in the mornings was to take dictation from the Squadron Leader. Although he was never directly irritable with her, his face usually wore a peevish look. Perhaps mornings were not his best time. Often she would have to ask him to repeat his words because of his habit of speaking fast with his back to her. He looked out across the parade-ground as if searching, all the while fiddling with a silver lighter and unlit cigarette. How she wished she owned those two items. My, she'd drive a hard bargain in exchange for those. He was always well-mannered, and she suspected there was kindness underneath all that bluster. She'd also read in a manual that he wasn't supposed to be kind to Germans. She did her job and kept her mouth shut.

Her shorthand was terribly out of practice. It stared up at her, defying her to read it back. Today, further aggravation came in the form of Reggie, intent on trying his charms on the new girl.

'Working for Wheeler of the WRAF knickers fame, I

see?' he smarmed, moving her papers and sitting on her desk corner. 'Anything you want, girl, come to old Reggie.'

'We know,' interrupted Renate. She had primed Ilse about his black marketeering. He'd done time but got swift promotions. Interesting.

Sometimes she had to work late. When large consignments came in for onward transmission to other parts of the British zone, the paperwork had to be done immediately. Renate covered for her sometimes because a curfew was in force and Ilse had to get back to her digs. The streets were dangerous places even if you weren't German. Many of the military were here against their wishes. They had wanted to go home long ago, and they took their frustration out on the Germans. If you got arrested for being out after time and your arresting soldier or interrogator was a German-hater, you were in dead trouble.

One evening as she passed down the corridor from her office, the store-room at the bottom was open and deserted. On the shelves were rows upon rows of airforce blue tunics and trousers. Quickly she glanced up and down the passage. Next moment a battledress top and trousers were in her hands, and she fled.

19

Frau Tannenbaum was by now virtually President of the Ilse Weinacht Fan Club. Ilse did, literally, bring home the bacon. Status was assured if you knew someone who knew someone who could get hold of something that was difficult to get. Items such as bacon and washing-powder came under this heading. To Ilse, Renate's mum was the woman of the moment. Working in the canteen as she did brought her in direct contact with the left-overs, and there were plenty of those from the officers' five-course meals. Sometimes not just the rind but whole rashers would be left on the plates, together with luscious pieces of fat discarded by the diner.

Today was Friday. 'Letter from America' morning, so it was a pleasant surprise to find the Squadron Leader relaxedly puffing on a cigarette. His air-force sleeves, controlled by means of silver arm bands, were resting on the desk, and furthermore he had a smile to spare for his secretary. The office of this normally restless man contained neither family photos nor personal knick knacks of any description.

The first letter was to Wheeler's Soviet equivalent, an equipment officer in Liga. The text discussed sale of vehicles to the Russians and the RAF's preference for payment in corn rather than roubles.

'Your home town, of course, Fräulein Weinacht.'

'Yes, sir.'

'Not been back.' It was more a statement than a question.

'No, sir. It is beyond the limit of the distance we are allowed to travel.'

He was silent.

When she returned to her office, boy did Birgit look suspicious. She darkly suspected Ilse's English-German expertise gave her clout with the boss.

'Everything all right, Fräulein Weinacht?'

'Yes thank you, Miss Fortesque.'

As the months passed Renate continued to win the unofficial 'Best-Dressed Female on the Camp' award, despite her wardrobe comprising one white blouse and a black skirt.

'It's a case of having bought good quality in normal times,' she explained to Ilse.

Birgit mooned after Wheeler, who, if he was aware, took absolutely no notice. According to the girl in the post-room, who told Renate, who informed Ilse, who neglected to tell Birgit, the letters from America ceased.

Apart from trips to other RAF camps in the British zone and an occasional trip east to do business with their allies in this four-pronged empire, Wheeler passed his time in the office. The avalanche of files never seemed to decrease either in volume or urgency. He let off steam by frequent visits to the mess, where his reputation was for knocking 'em back, a reference which did not only apply to drinks. Mostly he came away unscathed. His predilection was for starting a conversation involving two other people, into which he would toss a time bomb of a remark. When the argument was in full swing, he would slip away, leaving the combatants slugging it out and forgetful of who had stirred things in the first place.

'It's the boss's birthday today,' said Renate one morning. 'Apparently in England when it's someone's birthday there's cream cakes all round. Today – and you'll never believe this, Ilse – we're having his favourite for afters: apple crumble. Apparently one of Wheeler's superiors commandeered a house with an orchard! What do you think of that?'

'Well I th. . .' but Renate was not to be stopped so easily. Ilse gave up. She could see by the way her colleague's eyes glazed over and the settling back into the chair that she was in for an epic of a monologue.

'That takes me back. "Apple crumble". What emotive words. I remember a family holiday in England. Long before the war, this was. I see that Victorian pier as if it was yesterday. Promenading on the pier was all the thing. And the announcer said it so sweetly. Honeyed tones, that's what he had. Honeyed tones.' Renate said it a few more times. She seemed to like that phrase. Ilse drew breath but she was too late. Renate's roller-coaster of nostalgia rolled on, flattening Ilse into enjoying it.

"Luncheon is now being served at the south end of the pier. There will be roast beef and Yorkshire pudding, followed by apple crumble." It was the "apple crumble" bit that got me, but I never had the money. It would have been such a treat. I told Mother about it years later. She was so upset. "I wish I'd known," she said, "I'd have taken you." Now it's too late. I bet the pier's gone, and the announcer is probably dead. Missed opportunities. I had a literary flair and didn't do anything about it. And then the war put an end to my dreams. Don't you miss out on anything, Ilse. Do it now. Say it now, and no regrets later on.'

A crash. No need to look up to see who it was.

'Fräulein Weinacht, a minute of your time, please.'

Ilse grabbed the notepad that stood ever ready on the desk corner.

'No book. Just a word.' She followed in his imperious wake, wondering how much of this chauvinistic showmanship was a con and how much was real. Very little was real, she would imagine. Thankfully Birgit was absent from her perch, or she'd be explaining to her afterwards exactly what had been said. Birgit needed to be in the know so that she 'could run the office more efficiently.' That was her excuse.

Never a time-waster – he used time like a piece of valuable equipment – Wheeler came straight to the point.

'I need an interpreter this evening. Are you free?' What a laugh. Was she free? She was free every evening. Same meal of soup, and the highlight was having the electric bar on for five minutes if it was cold.

'I've invited some selected local dignitaries to the Pine Woods Club. It's important we don't delay any further about getting local government working again. I don't know how good their English is and my German's patchy, as you well know. Can you help out?' He took her long silence as a no.

'I'm sorry. It's just I thought as your grammar was so good, you'd automatically speak well in all situations.' Still she didn't know what to say. The Pine Woods Club. It was a hot potato amongst her people. The workers, the underclass, were lucky if they had a tarpaulin, yet the occupiers had their clubs with ballrooms, bands, gymnasia. He bumbled on.

'If it's clothes, Reggie'll be able to get something. What you're wearing at present would be admirable. It's a work occasion, not social,' he assured her.

'I didn't think Germans were allowed into the Pine Woods Club?'

'The small print allows fraternization in work situations. This is what this will be. We'd be using the conference-room. I think you'll find many in high places are in no position to throw the first stone. I've got plenty on them,' he finished meaningfully. She left the room totting up how many homeless would be able to sleep on the floor of their 'conference-room'.

Naturally, Ilse's social standing soared still further when Frau Tannenbaum saw Ilse go off with a British officer in a Mercedes. Hate and practicality fought a little battle in her provincial breast. Hate because these people had taken over her home, acceptance because she was a snob, and condoning of the situation because Ilse could get things for her. Ilse explained to her landlady that it was business. In doing so she was trying to calm her own unease. She wished she had had more time to think the thing through. Where was loyalty to be placed? Her boss? Her countrymen? Her own advancement?

After picking up two local officials, they drove for miles through fragrant pines. The polite silence was broken only occasionally by Wheeler's comments on the scenery.

The tyres slewed noisily on the gravel as they stopped outside a building – a hybrid between a hunting-lodge and over-large ski chalet. Ilse waited for the expected tanned ski instructor to leap boisterously towards them, but the scene remained sedate. Wheeler changed his mind, restarted the car and parked it round the rear next to the algae-green swimming-pool. Folding summer chairs of canvas and wood were dotted here and there. Shutters framed the small windows of the club.

Looking back, Ilse could not remember much about the two Germans. Wheeler eclipsed the evening, it was so different from his almost brutish approach during office hours. In his bookcase she'd seen the title of a book referring to personality. His name was on the cover. He was certainly a good advert – this evening, anyway – for his preachings. Despite the street wisdom she had acquired in recent years, she felt won over.

She translated into German Wheeler's enquiries as to what machinery would be needed to bring in the harvest. The present equipment was antiquated or kaput, and spare parts were unobtainable. He would see that tools were available. The two men must organize every able-bodied person, down to the last returning child evacuee, to go out and bring in the crops. The alternative was more people dead.

'Where are you from, Fräulein?' the bull-necked man with the built-in animosity asked Ilse.

'The eastern part,' said Ilse vaguely, a warning note in her voice that did not invite any follow-up to the question. This man was too curious in his glances and far too rounded in the flesh; she did not wish to give him any more information than was strictly necessary. She wondered how he came to look so sleek. Equally, he probably assumed she was sleeping with the boss. Moneyed male occupiers and starving Fräuleins added up to a neat little number, in his book.

She was glad when the evening was over and she was safely back in the company of her electric fire. But the episode didn't end there. Things rarely do.

That damn Reggie and his tom-tom information network. It was all round the camp next morning. Someone who knew someone who knew the Number One Louse had spotted her at the Pine Woods Club. If it had been wartime or the period directly after its end when emotions were running high, she well knew what sort of reprisals she might expect. The worst she encountered were the icy stares.

'A work assignment,' she explained to a puce-faced Birgit. It was the wrong thing to have said. It underlined how much more useful she was to Wheeler than his PA.

'Have you considered how much certain quarters would like to hear about this?' from the basin of the ladies' loo the voice threatened.

'I thought things were all right now.'

'You little innocent. Plenty of people would like your job,' hissed Birgit, sounding like a reincarnation of Frau Reinhardt. With her missile finding a direct hit, she swept imperiously from the cloakroom.

'Where angels fear to tread again,' muttered Ilse at the much older face that stared palely back at her in the mirror.

Suddenly there did not seem to be so many left-overs available from the kitchen. Ilse's fingertip sensitivity had been right all along. Now she had fallen between two stools; alienating her own countrymen and remaining unacceptable to the British. Fortunately she didn't get asked to the club again, but the damage had been done.

Normally effervescent, Ilse grew silent and insular. She had no social life, and she didn't want any. There was nowhere she wanted to go and no one she wished for as company.

Globally it was a troubled world. The harvest discussed at the Pine Woods Club failed. Other countries had problems supplying their own people, let alone allowing precious commodities to be exported to a former enemy. She caught a glimpse of an English newspaper. Banner headlines proclaimed the German people were in clover. How wrong could they be. Hunger oedema was endemic, people ran with open sores that never healed, streets were crime-riddled and administration was parlous. No word came from Michelle, only chilling news of what had been discovered at rehabilitation centres. The two councillors with whom Ilse had dined at the club were amongst those requested to view what had been done in the name of a political regime.

Heimstadt being the nucleus of the supply network, Ilse worked long hours. Wheeler came to depend more and more on the expertise of his young secretary with the old eyes. He contrived to help her without appearing to grant her special favours. A small box-room became vacant on the camp, and she moved in. It enabled her to work late without worry about the curfew and street safety.

Wheeler was complaining about the frayed edges of the prayer-mat in front of his desk.

'Order a mat from the stores, Ilse. Get rid of this one,' he said.

She understood his look by now which said, 'Here's a carpet.' Naturally she stored it on the floor of her room. Temporarily, of course, but she forgot to move it on.

One day she saw him on a train going east.

20

It seemed as if the whole world was on the move. All these people without an idea of whether there was anything or anyone left to go back to. Those who had not fulfilled their country's ideal of patriotism did not return. Suicide was preferable. Sadly, the hero's welcome took place more often in children's storybooks. In Central Europe at this time, seethed every conceivable nationality, all caught in a web of events outside their control. Now they were part of history's largest movement of human beings. They came home – different.

Ilse squeezed herself onto a train going to Liga. For many of the late-comers there was no room, it meant hanging onto door-handles and window-frames. In a borrowed brief-case – the boss had several gathering dust – were goodies for Mutti and Vati: dried milk, chocolate – how Mutti adored chocolate and how ghastly the pebbliness of the minuscule war ration – bacon – she and Renate were pals again – and vegetables which she had saved over the last two weeks from her own meals. Bringing food, sharing it, working for it was symbolic of love for family.

Elbowing onto the train was slow work. Ejection by the shovers who yelled 'no room' was swift. Squashed into the corner seat of a carriage was Wheeler. She tried to melt back into the crowd but he must already have seen her. However although he looked straight at her there was no hint of recognition on his face. Well, thank goodness, as today was Friday and she'd prepared for her expected absence by feigning illness yesterday. This time the crowd gave a huge heave which carried her into the corridor, where she tripped over protruding legs and a hen. Through the corner of a window she could still see him.

Dressed in wide-flannels, shirt-sleeves and dark tie, he had been studying a sheaf of typewritten pages. He was smoking, much to the annoyance of the grim-mouthed woman next to him, who pointedly made fanning movements with her hand. He took not the slightest notice. He looked grey and lonely. The absence of uniform made him look ordinary. In the non-cigarette hand was a pair of round horn-rimmed spectacles. He must need them for reading. The train bucked as it started up. She shrank back to where she would not be visible to him.

A few stops before Liga she got off the train. Some British airmen embarking greeted her. Firmly tucking the brief-case under her arm, she strode from the station, leaving the public road as soon as possible. She walked towards a lonely area of countryside. It was high and solitary, not at all like the picture-postcard terrain of further south. The ground was pitted with abandoned mine shafts, the sort convenient for throwing bodies down. It was known to be haunted. She came this way because she knew no one else would. Not unaccompanied, that is. Under the earth's crust was evil, and its vapours seemed to seep through. Thankfully there was no wind; but even so, pointed dead branches threatened like witches' fingers.

She lay down in the hollow created by a partially uprooted tree. Nestling against the earth, she turned her face to the ground so its whiteness might not be seen. She waited for nightfall, when she would walk across the zonal border that would take her into Soviet territory.

Stiff and terrified and under the doubtful protection of darkness, she walked across field and through forest until she reached the home that was no longer home. Crouching behind the hedge, she looked in at the lighted window. A huge, bulky woman was working at the sink where her mother had always stood. This creature had hair scraped back in a bun from a face that was like raw dough. Cast out from community life, Ilse felt as reviled as the wolves that encircled the town. She wanted to rush at the window and break it with her bare fists and get her fingers on that female's throat, a being that embodied all she had lost. But she crept away, not knowing the worst was to come.

Under cover of bushes further down the cart-track from her home, she waited for first light; a time, she reckoned, when drunkards had gone to ground, those looking for a good time were no longer in the mood and the workers were not yet on the go. They were in the last quarter of the moon. When the clouds parted, the sliver shone through, glinting on tracts of ruins that lay sealed off. Below her the bodies had gone, but there was accusation in the empty shells. In the eeriness something loose would flap every now and again.

Words hung in the air. 'Gone away. Gone away.'

Though the night was warm and dry, she shivered with the misery of it all. Could one begin again? She felt the howling winds of the fire-storm. She could see herself walking down the middle of that road, Katja on one arm, Michelle on the other. She could hear the squelch and slurp and sluice of filthy water from the burst sewer pipes.

The cold stones spoke. 'Dead. Dead.'

Katja was dead. Michelle? Nothing would ever be the same again. Along the passage from youth there is no return.

As the sky lightened, Ilse began her trek. Up and down, down and up tracks that corkscrewed over and around mounds of rubble. No one was about. She'd banked on this, but nestling amongst the food in her brief-case was a gun. Herr Tannenbaum, aghast at her reckless plan, had made her take his gun. If she was stopped and questioned she had none of the necessary papers. These could have been obtained at a price from Reggie, but that really would have placed her in his power. He would know her secret.

Everywhere was in utter ruin. Forced-labour workers from the east roamed the land, intent on pillage and revenge. Only by sheer miracle did she finally reach the last known address of her parents, which Hans had given her. She knocked on the scarred door of the middle house of the only three still standing in the street. Makeshift curtains moved faintly at a glassless window. Did she imagine it, or did someone peer out at her?

'Mutti,' she whispered, placing her mouth close to the wood, and hoping with all her heart that after seven months she had come home. The door scraped back slowly. In the opening was a woman, bent-shouldered, piteously thin, with eyes that seemed to be growing dim. The woman gazed at the young airman on her doorstep, then her face lit up as it was transformed with joy. It was as if God had turned on a light.

'Ilse, my Ilse.'

Feelings exploded in her chest as she held her mother tightly.

She did not know how long she stood there, but

when she opened her eyes, over her mother's shoulder she saw Vati, gaunt faced, deeply lined around the mouth, with his suit hanging from a once-tubby figure, coming towards her, his arms outstretched. A smell of cauliflower filled the one room and Tante Frieda put down her knitting.

21

In the unexcitement of a Monday morning, and back in her niche as a worker bee in the hive, she toiled at her unresponsive shorthand. Much had happened since she jotted it down last Thursday. Monday mornings ought to be banned. They were a health hazard, she reckoned. But then there would be black Tuesdays.

Renate entered the room softly. Everything she did was gentle. She obeyed the age-old philosophy of nothing mattering very much and most things not mattering at all.

'How's your cold?' she asked.

'Oh, much better, Renate. Much better.'

'Good.' The door panels shuddered as Freddie Wheeler dealt with it as he dealt with all barriers that barred his entry. Birgit teetered in his wake. The office dust settled. Renate grinned.

'No doubt hoping today's the day he undoes her bun, removes her glasses and says, "Why, Fräulein Fortesque, you're beautiful. Why have I never noticed before?"' giggled Renate.

'Probably,' said Ilse, her mind elsewhere.

Birgit re-emerged. Stopping by Ilse's desk she said reverently, 'Squadron Leader Wheeler would like a word.'

'Thank you,' said Ilse, privately thinking, bugger Birgit. Why doesn't she grow up? Where's she been all her life? Men aren't pieces of Meissen to be owned and displayed in a cabinet.

Wheeler waved at the chair in front of his desk. His face was stern. She felt as if she were in the presence of the headmaster. He leaned towards her, his hands planted on the desk.

'May I enquire as to your health, Fräulein Weinacht?' he said sweetly.

'My cold's a lot better, thank you,' she replied, rather surprised. The ticks of a mahogany mantelpiece clock filled the silence.

'And may I enquire as to what you were doing in an RAF uniform at Heimstadt Station?' he asked, even more sweetly.

'Oh, uh, I didn't think you'd seen,' she mumbled. This was it. Job up the spout.

'I don't like to do the predictable,' he said, glaring. But somehow he did not frighten her.

'Are your parents alive?' she asked him.

'No.'

'Would you visit them if they were?'

'I'd swim through a lake of fire.'

She didn't say any more. He broke a pencil in two.

'Ilse.' It was the first time he'd used her Christian name. 'I'd come with you if I could. I sometimes have business in that area. But I can't, I'd be court-martialled for condoning this deception. I don't want to know any more. I don't know about it. Do you understand?'

'Yes, sir.' She left him staring hard at a dried-out cactus on the window sill.

Birgit was importantly sorting out the post when Ilse returned to their office. It was always performed with much huffing and blowing, the implication being that this job really was beneath her but she did it for them because they couldn't be trusted to do it as well as she could.

'Tut,' she exclaimed in annoyance. 'Private and confidential.' She held the envelope up to the light, her face registering disapproval at her entry being barred to its contents. She bustled into Wheeler's office bearing the offending missive. Ilse wondered if the letter was from America. She felt a wave of hatred for this woman who was tying Freddie up like a knotted hankerchief. *Oh God, here we go, the symptoms. . . . No use getting too fond.* He was kind to her, that was all. He'd go back to England. A few letters may be. Then nothing.

'These people must be in a bad way,' said Renate, reading out a few lines from the list she was typing. 'Sixty tons DDT, twenty tons insecticide, two and a half million units insulin, six hundred tons general medical supplies.'

Ilse wandered over to her colleague's desk. The name of the camp stared up at her. No, it didn't stare up at her. It hit her right between the eyeballs.

'You OK?' queried Renate, looking at her colleague curiously.

'I'm fine, thanks,' said Ilse, returning to her desk, where she hardly got anything done for the rest of the day.

Over the next few years, she went regularly to see her parents. As her boss knew about these escapades, she didn't risk pushing her luck by taking time off work. She chose a Saturday, finding Sunday morning an especially deserted morning for picking her way across Liga.

Once, she went out to Michelle's place of work. As the camp was outside her permitted distance of travel she donned the RAF uniform. She now owned two uniforms and a false moustache. It had been an especial pleasure to pinch a Soviet officer's uniform from the washing line of her former home, and she put it to good use in the danger zone. But she never got anywhere near Michelle's camp. Large white notices said 'DANGER TYPHUS'. Sick at heart, she backed off and went home. A small door in her mind had a special label, *closed*. Then came the bombshell.

Morning dictation, and Ilse mechanically jotted down the shorthand, It was only at the end of the final letter that she realized what she had written down.

> 'Dear Sir, I am in receipt of your letter of 4 December and confirm I shall report at RAF Beisee on 5 January to take up the new post.'

There was some waffle and then a 'Yours faithfully', at which he swung round, perhaps to gauge her reaction. Too late. The pain, not unlike someone removing your finger-nails, came suddenly. By the time he had turned from his usual scanning of the parade-ground, she had her facial expression under control and her feelings neatly folded away. His 'That'll be all today, Ilse,' was rather quiet.

'Thank you,' she said, 'I'm so sorry to hear the news.' She wouldn't look at his face and left quickly.

Flinging her book and papers onto the desk, she fled for the sanctity of the ladies' loo – thank God it was empty – and cried. Then she picked up the bar of white soap that in early days had held her spellbound, washed her hands, patched up her shiny face, and returned to work.

Obviously Birgit had heard. Her face was distraught, and under the weight of tears her mascara branched out in all directions just like elongating spider legs.

'And we were getting on *so* well. He even bought me a drink,' she wailed.

Renate was not naturally bitchy, but Birgit had the talent for dredging up the worst in most people.

'Big-hearted Freddie buys everyone a drink. Perhaps he bought you a bigger one than everyone else?' She replied, and plonked a coffee in front of her suffering room-mate.

Birgit's bun chose this moment to unravel. 'Now look what you've done?' Birgit shook the coffee-drenched hair, causing it to splatter the notice-board.

'Oh shut up,' snapped Ilse.

'I don't know what's got into you two. We'll probably get someone a lot more placid,' said Renate calmly.

Birgit gave up. She was next for the cloakroom. The people waiting for interviews in the outer office showed not a flicker of interest as a WRAF lady looking as though she had been interfered with sprinted through the hall.

Ilse helped Freddie to sort out the files before his replacement came. She paused nostalgically over the underwear and loo paper files. It seemed another lifetime when they had giggled like schoolchildren over the vagaries of supply trying to deal with demand.

'I'm not far away, you know. If you need help you know where to find me,' he said across an open filing-cabinet drawer. Two of the drawers were open at the same time. The cabinet teetered dangerously. Freddie steadied it.

'Whew, that was a close call.'

'Things won't be the same,' she smiled.

'We'll keep in touch,' he replied. How she hated those words. 'Keep in touch' always seemed to be the forerunner to losing touch.

22

Things weren't the same. The camp joiner didn't need to fix the door quite so often and Birgit wittered unbearably, making sure the community suffered with her. Even the batman with his long Spanish-style moustache missed the bombastic boss. His was the task of checking that sir's morning cup of tea was just right.

'That'll do for gaffer,' he said every morning without fail, after trailing his flowing moustache in the hot liquid as he checked it for strength and temperature.

On the last day Freddie handed her an envelope.

'Ilse, will you type this up tomorrow? It's blank but I've signed it at the bottom. Just in case you might need it.' Later that night in her room she opened the envelope. Inside was the handwritten draft of a testimonial, together with a blank form used when submitting a reference to the German Labour Office. The brief instructions were in German and English. She was to fill in the spaces. His signature in black ink was scrawled along the bottom. It was unusual for an employee to have a copy unless they applied for one.

> Miss Ilse Weinacht is employed at this Group Headquarters in the capacity of a shorthand typist. During her time here she has given complete satisfaction. She has a thorough

mastery of the English language, and is an exceptionally speedy shorthand typist.

She is endowed with a charming personality, is willing and courteous at all times, and has good educational qualifications and a sound intellectual background. I have no hesitation in recommending her to any future employer.

Next morning she was at her office desk early in order to be alone when she typed up the testimonial. No such luck. Reggie had chosen this morning to do his usual pilfering. This time it was reams of paper, which he would sell on at inflated prices. Bad-manneredly he put his head close to Ilse's in order to have a good look at what she was typing. Fortunately only the heading was visible.

'Somebody being given the boot then, my old love?' he said gleefully, rubbing his hands together. Others' misfortunes cheered him greatly.

'Sorry, confidential,' she smiled. She didn't want this man as an enemy. He scared her; he had no scruples. But then, did she?

The air seemed to rustle in panic as Birgit, well-scrubbed and bustling, came in ready for the fray. Not looking as though he'd experienced a day's starvation, Reggie sauntered gangly-legged to her desk. Ilse capitalized on the moment by locking the unfinished reference in her top desk drawer.

'Got over the dashing Squadron Leader yet, sweetie-pie?' smirked Reggie.

Birgit didn't appear insulted. For all her public histrionics her skin seemed remarkably thick.

'Love 'em and leave 'em,' she retorted bravely. Perhaps she'd have to cut her losses now and settle for second-best. No use offending Reggie – after all, he supplied her with silk stockings and chocolate.

'I gather our dashing officer has already cut quite a swath at Beisee,' said Reggie, thudding his heels against Birgit's desk.

'Oh?' said Birgit with more than a little curiosity. She never gave up hope and was still thirsty for news.

'My network informs me of some very interesting goings-on.'

Ilse stopped typing. Intently she studied her next file. Good job her hair had at last grown long enough to cover her ears. She was sure they were standing out on stalks, hanging on Reggie's next words. Certain of his audience and tickling their curiosity like trout in a stream, Reggie paused.

'Oh, do get on with it,' said Birgit in extreme irritation.

'Wrecked a bar.'

'Wrecked a bar!' Ilse couldn't stop herself blurting out.

'Oh, not as immune as we make out,' he sneered.

'Doesn't seem in character, that's all,' muttered Ilse.

'Rubbish. Not in character? I'll say it's in character. Never happier than when he's propping up or smashing up a bar. Drank six of us under the table one night. Not a sign until he got out of the door. Found him next morning in a flower-bed, talking to a bunch of petunias or some such.'

'So?' said Birgit dismissively. She sniffed, and powdered her nose.

Reggie looked at Ilse, disappointed at her lack of reaction. That lady sure was a cool one, he thought. Too cold for his liking. Now Birgit.... Get through that bossiness – actually it quite turned him on – which she wore like a corset, and you could find quite a little spitfire. He lit a cigarette and stared hard at Ilse. Couldn't make her blush. What a waste of time, and he'd heard these German women were dying for men like him. Must be something wrong with her.

'Oh yes, Wheeler likes to make out he's so pure. You know, Baptist church-goer, mother-loving, nice to his sisters and all that crap but you see 'im with a drink down 'im. He's really screwed up this time. Woman, I expect. Perhaps it's back on with his Yankee piece. Like a raging bull, 'e was. No one dared to go near 'im. Joint a shambles when he'd finished.'

Reggie finished the last of his cigarette, stubbed it out in a flowerpot, chucked Birgit under the chin and bent his foul nicotined head next to hers.

'Lunch, maybe? You could do worse.'

Ilse had become addicted to danger. She positively looked forward to pushing her luck. As the six-kilometre travel ban was still imposed on Germans, today she donned her RAF outfit. The freedom of not being German and not being a woman was an elixir.

She got off the train at Beisee, checked her home-made moustache was in place, and strode purposefully to her destination.

It was Saturday. The offices of RAF Beisee were deserted save for Wheeler, who was working on a philosophy book he'd started before the war. Concentration was easier here than at his quarters, which had thin walls and an over-helpful batman. He struggled for words. It all used to come so easily. Damn. Damn. He lit an umpteenth cigarette and looked out of the window for inspiration.

'What the hell?' he thundered. He'd no sooner swept round his desk to the door when it was flung open for him with the kind of force he used himself.

'De-da,' said the vision, sweeping off its moustache. 'What the....'

'Fancy a drink?' said the apparition, spiriting a beer bottle from its tunic.

'I'll give you a drink. What right have you to come here and sweep a man off his feet?' He grabbed her and gave her a great smacking kiss on the lips, which like a miracle slowly changed to something that wasn't just good mates. One hand stroked the back of his neck, the other felt the roughness of his flying jacket. It didn't seem either could make a decision to draw apart.

When they drew breath to speak he said, 'My old mother always said, "Treat every girl like your sister and you can't go far wrong." You don't feel a bit like my sister.'

'Well, that's a relief, I must say. I don't expect your sisters went around in men's clothing propositioning men.' In his eyes she saw a light that was reserved for her only. She had never seen him look like that. The laughter and then the tension was delicious. If only this moment could last for ever, the look in his eyes....

'You know what my mother said?'

'I don't think I want to know.'

'She warned me about men like you.'

'And did you come all this way to see me?'

'Certainly not.'

'You're like the damn mermaid on the Lorelei. One minute you're there seducing me in your androgynous clothing, the next a wave's gone over you and you've disappeared. Give a man a break.'

She laughed. 'Work?' and she nodded to his desk.

'A book. I can't get going at all.'

'Your first?'

'No, I did two after university.'

'University,' she said wistfully. 'Oh, I'd love to have

had the chance, but they don't think much to spending money on a girl's education. They just think you'll do the usual.'

'Will you do the usual?'

'Are you offering the usual?'

'I'm not a good bet. I'm very difficult, you know.'

'And did you wreck the bar because you didn't get me?'

'How. . .? Oh Reggie's jungle drums again, I suppose. Certainly not. Merely artistic temperament.'

They stood looking at each other. Neither was looking for trouble, and here it was in the guise of each other. He took her hand, drawing her near again. Her eyes drew him.

'My answer is "yes",' she said.

'I haven't asked you,' he said.

'Can you afford to pay for any more wrecked bars?'

'Not on a squadron leader's pay.'

'Well then?'

They gave up the fight, allowing a power greater than themselves to take over.

The following weekend she went home to Mother. It was at times like this that Mutti fetched out the chocolate box – the one with the white kitten with a red ribbon around its neck. This old chocolate box had always been around although lately it had not been full. If either Ilse or her mother could get into a cigarette queue and get lucky, they could exchange them for stock for the chocolate box. When Ilse was a child, her mother would sit with her before bedtime. They'd say a prayer to the *Liebe Gott*, then Ilse could choose a chocolate. After such habits and the inadequate war diet it was a wonder she had teeth.

'I told you, didn't I, that Squadron Leader Wheeler

had been transferred to Beisee? I thought there'd be a replacement but that dreadful Reggie's in charge. Luckily Birgit gets most of the attention.'

'Oh dear,' said Mutti. She was sad. Her Ilse was different.

'I miss him. And now they've started posting people back to England.'

'Yes,' said Mutti, waiting.

'I think we were testing each other. You know, seeing if there was anything in it. It was well-known round camp he wasn't the marrying sort.'

Mutti nodded.

'I didn't want to get married and I didn't want to leave this country but. . .'

'Love's a powerful thing. I gave up my country for your father. The pain comes later, but eventually you have to settle.' Mutti's eyes had glazed over. She was no longer in the room. She was eighteen again, and he was crazy about her.

'I always thought I'd come back here,' said Ilse, miserably fiddling with a hankerchief.

'We won't last for ever and Tante Frieda's going into a nursing home. We don't want to think of you on your own. Is he a sensible man?'

'I don't know. He's very good at getting things done. I hear he's rather wild, although I've never seen it.'

'Do you trust him?'

'Yes.' Then Ilse perked up. 'And I can always visit you regularly.'

'Let's enjoy today,' said her mother. She didn't mention Vati hadn't been well or the political rumours.

Ilse made a bad miscalculation. She was in love and going to England and naturally she wanted to tell the world about it. How she wished she'd kept her mouth shut. She'd still be earning. RAF Heimstadt was gradually handing more of the administration back to local Germans and posting British personnel back home. As the work-load decreased, Ilse's position became redundant. Reggie and Birgit enjoyed telling her that.

'You see, my old love, as you're going to England anyway, we thought you wouldn't mind too much being given the first heave-ho. By the way, I've done quite a bit of train-spotting these last few years.' He flashed a yellow-toothed smile and slapped her matily on the back.

She'd behaved like an immature schoolgirl showing off. Now here she was back on the streets, combing the suburbs for a room, for which she would have to pay black-market prices. She found one, a squalid dump of a place; and discovered how quickly savings go down when you're not earning – and how socially unacceptable you are when you're unemployed and living in a bed-sit at the wrong end of town. She badgered the Emigration Headquarters for her papers. By the time she got them, would Freddie, known to everyone but her as a hell-raising womanizer, have changed his mind?

BOOK III

BOOK III

23

About all she could remember was the grey and blue check suitcase sliding from one side of the cabin to the other. There had been one remaining berth, though it meant sharing a cabin with a man. She and her roommate were so seasick and their concentration on their own physical distress was so total, that if they met again they would not recognize each other. However, he recovered sufficiently to wish her luck when they docked in Harwich.

From the ship's railings, and feeling an unromantic greenish-yellow, she scanned the quayside for the familiar figure. There he was, impatient as ever, pacing up and down, hands behind his back, just as if he was inspecting his men.

'Freddie. Freddie,' she shouted, willing him to pick her out of the crowd that swelled dangerously towards the edge as the ship drew nearer the dockside, bringing home its cargo of servicemen to be reunited with their loved ones. Everyone was craning forward, desperately searching out that special face.

'She's come! She's really come,' she heard him yell.

It seemed ages before the boat finally came to rest and they were at last allowed to totter down the swaying gangway. The planks and rope across the chasm were symbolic of the bridge between two worlds now no longer at war, but gradually healing the wounds with the best ointment of all – a love affair.

There was no problem about waiting around for the hold to be emptied. Everything she owned was in the small suitcase. Unbelievably it had been a leaving present from Birgit and Reggie.

She looked at the sky. 'Wish me luck.'

She didn't realize she'd said it aloud until an Australian voice loaded with images of cattle stations and macho saloons said, 'Good on ya, mate. He's a lucky bloke.'

He grinned. She did too. God, she was happy and scared that she was. It couldn't last. Good times, bad times. Nothing lasted. When had she felt like this? Probably pre-war Liga and the feel of the bobbly cobbles beneath her thin evening shoes. The passionate discussions of home-going opera fanatics. The smell of wine as pleasure oozed from buildings. Then, as the mists rose up, the homeward stroll along the river bank. Boisterous culture swirled around her and whoever was flavour of the moment. They seemed to have all the time in the world for romantic evenings and youthful silliness.

What is it about a certain mind and body that makes all else irrelevant? As his arms closed around her she was taken into a world of clean woody haircream, mintiness and cigarette tang. Surely this was the harbour for which she had been searching?

'I was worried you might go off with Reggie,' he whispered to her earlobe.

'I nearly did. You never gave me chocolate or silk stockings, just practical things like a room and a carpet,' she replied tartly.

'I have a warehouseful just waiting for you. I wanted to be sure it was my body you wanted and not food.'

'Don't kid yourself, Freddie Wheeler. I'm only here for the English cooking.' She picked up her suitcase.

'Ilse Weinacht, stop right now being so independent. You trying to emasculate me already or something?' He grabbed the luggage from her.

'Twit,' she chuckled, taking his hand.

They walked from the quay. A young woman – twentyish – was sitting at the wheel of his car.

'Meet Susan, my chauffeuse.'

Susan nimbly sprang out of the seat to shake hands with Ilse. She looked curiously at this German woman who had finally stirred Freddie Wheeler from his bachelorhood.

'May I welcome you to England, Miss Weinacht?' Her handshake was firm, her smile friendly and accepting.

'Thank you. I'm so glad to be here.'

Susan opened the car door for her, then nipped round to assist the Squadron Leader. 'Sir,' she saluted.

The car purred through meadows bursting with buttercups and cow parsley. The full glories of an English summer-time stepped out to welcome its visitor from Armageddon.

Freddie had arranged a room for her in RAF Petersham's neighbouring town until they could move into quarters nearer the camp. Freed at last from the restrictions of race laws and curfews, they got down to the serious business of courtship. Amid soporific air that induced heavy-liddedness and yawning early in the evening, rolling green hills and warm-stoned houses, they took the exquisite journey common to all lovers: the unwrapping of the parcel they were purchasing for life.

They were to be found, their heads bent close and talking as if there was too little time, in small narrow-streeted towns whose houses' upper storeys leant wickedly over jostling pavements. They strolled arm in arm in spas where military men with gout retired, flowers crammed every window-box and square, fountains played, shops stayed open and people planned for the future. He bought her a new dress, her first since before the war. It was black and lilac and fell in sheafs of luxurious silk.

Only occasionally did the past intrude. They attended evening dances in the mess, and when one of the tall handsome ex-bomber pilots asked her to partner him, before long he would ask the inevitable.

'Germany,' she would answer.

'Where?'

In time she learned not to say Liga. This word brought a strange look to her questioner's face and she would sense his desire to get away. For the remainder of the evening she would feel the curious eyes upon her. Her father's advice came back to her: *Speech is silver, silence is gold.*

Freddie in his uniform and Ilse in her black and lilac dress married in a registry office. Two passing locals acted as their witnesses. After the ceremony the modest group stood on the steps in the sunshine.

The registrar turned to Ilse. 'Are your in-laws alive?'

'No.'

He nodded approvingly. 'You're lucky.'

Married quarters turned out to be a tiny cottage, hidden behind shrubbery, on the edge of the sleepiest village green. From the privy, cheek by jowl to the back door, one could watch the children going to school. This rustic loo had sitting tenants – dinner-plate-sized black spiders. Nothing would persuade them to give up their squatters' rights, and it wasn't long before their relatives heard about this desirable residence. Water came by way of a long-handled pump in the kitchen, and cooking was performed on a hotplate which made the adjacent work surface dangerously alive.

After Freddie had cycled off to work, Ilse's daytime companions were a horse in the high-grassed field behind and a cat called Bonk. The latter was large, black and unblinking. All day he sat on the sill, staring into the kitchen, which unnerved Ilse, who hadn't been brought up with pets. In return for food, he offered twenty-four-hour attention and total loyalty, until the fishmonger offered him a better deal. When Bonk left for his fishy paradise, all parties were happy.

Behind the privy they found an ancient though serviceable deck-chair, its canvas permeated with mould. Ilse set it up against the horse field fence, whilst Freddie fetched their one kitchen chair. Over Ilse's head spread a canopy of elderberry and honeysuckle, and the sun filtering through their leaves formed dappled patterns on her dress. She looked up at him perched on the high seat, his foot propped on the garden table in front of him, a cigarette casually slotted between his fingers.

'Just now you look like my mother,' he smiled.

'How old were you when she died?'

'Twenty. Part way through university. I had to go back later and finish the course. I think I must have had a breakdown.'

'How long before you got better?'

'I don't think you ever do get better. I went away. It's not home any more when your Mam's gone. Sisters aren't the same. I've lot of those.'

'You never talk about your family.'

'I suppose we all split up and went to live in far-flung places. Although I wasn't the favourite I was mad about her. We went for drives in the country in my first car, but she was never the same after Bill – that's my eldest brother – was killed a couple of days before the end of the first war. More people die of a broken heart than anything else.'

She kissed his cheek. 'Darling Freddie. Let's go inside.'

Ilse also missed Renate who had returned to her home town in the east. She had been such an anchor in the shifting world of the ruins. But they kept in touch. Every week Ilse wrote to Mutti and Vati and regularly sent things they liked, such as English coffee and marzipan. Her parents were back in their own home. Vati was retired, and they met up with the remnants of their friends who had made it through the war.

She tried to visit them every couple of years but travelling was tense. On arrival and departure in the eastern part of Germany she had to report to the police station. She always worried there would be political turbulence and the borders would close whilst she was there.

> Dearest Renate,
> My deepest sympathy on your loss. Your dear mother – how could I ever repay her kindness? I was starving and she got me food. She didn't even know me. Why oh why is it the sweetest and best who go too early? I shall never forget how much you helped me in those early days at Heimstadt. I can't bear to think what you must be feeling at this time.
> My love as always,
> *Ilse*

> Dear Renate,
> I don't know when would be the right time

to ask you. Mary was born this spring. Not long ago, in fact, and we ask whether you would consider being her godmother. We would very much like to call her Mary Renate.

It is unfortunate for me that in this tiny village where we now live there is the most luscious cake-shop imaginable. Whilst pregnant I was a frequent visitor to the establishment. Freddie said it was like going for a walk with a full-rigged sailing-ship. He always looked so proud of his huge Frau. I can picture your face now, Renate. You can't visualize me as anything other than a matchstick.

Mary, just like Freddie, is impatient to get things over and done with. She started coming as the ambulance was half-way across the River Emmett. Freddie was on night duty at the camp. The nurse really ticked him off when he telephoned to ask about the baby. 'Just a normal baby,' she said.

I can't feed her myself, I've still got that breast infection. Legacy, I presume, of the years of bad diet. It's a miracle Mary's a healthy child.

You can't plan life, can you? We've found a lovely place here and now it's time to move on. The RAF are encouraging a lot of the older men to go. Even if Freddie stayed to the bitter end he wouldn't get a full pension. He hasn't done enough years. He's madly going to interviews for lecturerships but so far no luck. Either they tell him he's too old, or a local man gets the position. He's very down.

If only you could come for the christening on 15 April? The Wall. Always the Wall. You one side, me the other.

My prayers are with you. My love as ever.

Ilse

Ilse wrote again to the Missing Persons Inquiry Office. The letter came back. They were, they said, 'unable to trace the above-mentioned Dr Michelle Weidel.'

Often Freddie stayed at the mess for several beers before coming home. As he cycled up to the front gate, Mary's gurgling and waving beneath her red bee-net lifted his depression.

At last he got a job. A college in an industrial northern town could use his skills. The local man, poised to land the vacancy, made a mistake at his interview. This was Freddie's forty-sixth attempt at securing employment in civvy street. The family moved north, their idyll foundering a little as responsibility engulfed them.

During the ceaseless round of country clubs and dances in the mess, Freddie had warned Ilse, 'It won't always be like this you know.'

She hadn't believed him, but when the paternal umbrella of the RAF came down she thought about what he had said. It was time to take stock. They worked out their financial assets. It hardly took up one sheet of paper.

'Oh well, no clothes for a while. Thank goodness we've both already got good-quality stuff,' said Ilse, and as she said it she thought of Renate's philosophy.

'And no car,' said Freddie firmly.

'Oh.' Ilse looked disappointed. She'd got used to a car and chauffeuse.

'No,' said Freddie even more emphatically. 'I once bought a car on the never-never, and that's exactly what it turned out to be. I never stopped paying for it, even after I'd sold the damn thing. Cash on the nail or not at all,' he added from his packing-case seat.

Ilse was back to life without chairs. They didn't have any, or the money to pay for any.

'Never mind. This is all ours,' she said, blissfully allowing her gaze to wander around the bare front room of their between-the-wars semi-detached house. 'Our first home. I've never owned anything. Back home, people usually rent. Vati was an exception. He inherited.'

Freddie smiled, sharing the enjoyment of ownership. He reached for his lighter, then remembered he'd given up smoking when Mary was born. Oh well, he'd have a drink later. Perhaps not. He could only afford a half-pint a week now.

24

Dear Renate,

... Mary starts school soon. Thank goodness. It's like having a miniature Freddie around the place. They have a storm of a row and then the sun shines again and they've forgotten what it was all about. I'm looking out of the French window now – oh, Renate these moors are bleak, I think you're got to be born to them – I can just see Freddie, his flying jacket flapping open, standing talking to Mary. They're under the pear tree and it's looking pretty serious. He's given her a patch of garden to cultivate but she wants more. The latest demand is a pond and terrapin breeding.

It's so different from Liga and Heimstadt. When the smog settles just beyond the back fence it stays for days. The desolation seeps into your bones. To save our sanity the women around here get together for coffee mornings. Gossip session, really. Whoever is absent gets talked about mercilessly. I've been pigeon-holed as "that German woman".

Freddie's always late home and is speechless with tiredness when we meet. Mary and I are cashing in on the time before she goes to school. She's inherited the family addiction to tea and cream cakes. She finds our trips to the great department store in Masefield a real treat. The highlight of the visit is their ladies' loo with its pink carpet, soft music and wall-length mirrors.

One day she stared into the mirror, 'Mummy do you think I'll ever be beautiful?' she said.

It was not a good day for me and I said, 'We'll have to wait and see.'

Renate, her little face looked so crumbled and disappointed. It wasn't the answer she wanted from her mum. She wanted reassurance and I didn't give it. Why didn't I? Have I become that hard? . . .

Dear Renate,
. . . If only we could meet up. They let the older people out to visit but it's a long time to wait . . . Freddie works all the time and Mary has just started school. It is so difficult to find my own time. Does the wonderful whirlwind courtship always become shopping, cooking, washing up, waving them off in the morning, waiting for them to come home etc. etc. etc? What *is* it about us women that makes us put duty before our own needs? Is it part of nature's grand design? A way of ensuring the young are nurtured up until independence, up until they have to pay their first electricity bill and realize baths are not free? You must know, Renate. Your wise sayings from our office days always come back to me.

I know looking after a family is supposed to be a woman's most fulfilling role, but boy does the brain stagnate when the actual discipline of going out into the world to earn one's daily bread is taken away. One feels always on the outside of people's lives looking in. Freddie and Mary tell me all about their day. I wait to be asked about mine. I shouldn't hold my breath. They're tired, I know. I understand what you say about "footloose and fancy-free" not being all it's cracked up to be, but aren't we falling into the old trap – someone else has always got a better deal? Aren't we a silly pair? Still, I wish this rage would go away. It's like a chained tiger. Oh well, back to the sewing-machine. I'm making a jacket for Mary out of my grey coat. Lovely-quality material . . .

Dear Renate,
. . . the red poppies are out – all sprinkled in amongst the grasses and daisies on the roadside bank. I think about things – don't you? – when I see them . . . about time and change and where we all are. Freddie works too hard. He always seems to be trying to prove himself. It's awful to see responsibility take the joy out of a man. Can you imagine even Freddie getting sober-suited and grey? Life's like a marathon, isn't it? You start off full of hope, your muscles all fresh and vibrant. Half-way along the pain's killing you and you've a stitch in your side; and when you near the end, like Mutti and Vati, you wonder if you've enough in you to cross the finishing-line.

I've started a job. German translations for a second-hand furniture dealer. Not quite another Reggie, but nearly. I can't see Birgit and Reggie with children. Do you think they'll inherit their qualities? The imagination boggles. Going out to work has caused ructions, I can tell you! Freddie didn't mind, so long as it didn't interfere with the way the household was run, and Mary hates coming home to an empty house, and I'm always tired. Mary's a sweetie with her dad, but with me, well, we never seem to get on the same wavelength.

One evening she was a real poppet and came to meet me off the bus. Somehow we missed each other because I got off at the stop further down. She was so disappointed. I was worn out, Freddie had had too many beers, and an argument was brewing. Oh Renate, I didn't even think to thank her or say how sorry I was that we missed each other. I was careful to look out for her in future, but she never came again. Do you think it's that we saw too many things during the war that a human being ought never to see? Does it stop us feeling deeply again? The things that are so important to Mary seem trifling to me. They don't teach you how to be a mother do they? . . .

Dear Renate,
. . . Birgit can't still be carrying the torch for Freddie. We all fantasize. Best cure is get the dream. She'd find the dashing parade-ground Freddie a far cry from the everyday one. The *Alltag*, Mutti would call it.

Congratulations about your poetry. Will you sent me a copy? I'll send you the money. At last your dream came true. You see, Renate, if you wait long enough and never let go of the wanting. . . . Hark at me talking like this to you!

You warned me about anti-German feeling, but love does blind you for a time. You've got to be in love to even think about giving up your country. I must admit I've been lucky. People have been so good. On the odd occasions when it may have happened, perhaps it's just me being paranoid.

Coincidentally there's a teacher at Mary's school who has the same name as someone in high office in the government. It's an unusual name. Like all mothers, I'm ambitious for Mary. One day I dolled myself up and visited her school to see how she was coming along.

'She's twentieth,' said her teacher – Renate, there are only twenty-one in the class!

'Oh, but she tries so hard,' added the teacher consolingly. My foot. She enjoyed telling me. I went home half the size. It is customary for gold star winners to receive a sweet. Funny how this teacher has always just run out when Mary wins one – which isn't often . . .

Dear Renate,
. . . I didn't really understand how you felt when your mother died. I tried to but you can't until it happens to you. I thought my journey through wartime Germany had

taught me all about suffering, but nothing compares to this. There seems nowhere to run. Vati died before Christmas. He always said, "Think of me when you see the evening star." Oh I do. One evening in December I walked to the church. I hoped to find comfort. The church is some way from the village and there is no street lighting. It was so dark and that God-forsaken wind never stops howling over these moors. The church was shut and deserted. I ran home. Oh, the loneliness.

Our lives seem to be a solitary confinement inside our skins, with no one *really* knowing exactly how we feel. Darling Freddie and Mary. They look at me miserably, not knowing how to reach me. Mary and I made the Christmas cake. I almost couldn't go through with it. Finally, Freddie quite rightly, said, 'You'll have to pull yourself together.'

The doctor's given me some tablets. What a relief. They're wonderful. They block out the pain of feeling . . .

Dear Renate,
. . . Is it really two years since I've written? Forgive me. And you kept on and on writing to try and cheer me. I think I must have had some kind of breakdown. That word summons up all kinds of visions of mental institutions and strait-jackets, but it's nothing like that, is it? You go on as normal. People say, "Isn't she taking it well?" and yet inside you feel so ill and every nerve end is screaming, "Take me away from all this." Those tablets, so pleasurable at first, blocked out what I

couldn't bear. Then they had me by the throat, taking over my life. I was so nasty, I thought Freddie would leave. He stayed but drank more.

As you can see, we've moved south. Freddie took early retirement – colleagues younger than him were dropping dead with heart attacks. We're near to the sea and Mary is working in horticulture nearby . . .

As you say, sooner or later, a person's got to settle. We never could in the north. We tried, but everything seemed to go wrong. Even the house had bad vibes – the couple before us divorced. Here in the south the area was home to the Saxons – my own tribe – and of course we're handier for Germany. Oh Renate, I read between the lines what you are trying to tell me. Do you think it will happen in our lifetime?

25

'Oh Ilse, this damn back's painful this morning,' said Freddie, holding his back, an agonized expression on his face. Ilse looked up from the Sunday roast beef she was cooking to where Freddie sat at the kitchen table by the window of their bungalow by the sea.

'You know you really shouldn't have carried all those bucketfuls of stones. You forget you're not twenty. You and Mary are always showing off to each other. I'll rub some cream in tonight.'

The back pain didn't go away. Freddie just learned to live with it. Mary came home every weekend. On her walk from the station she sometimes met her parents on their way to the shops. What a sweet picture they made: her mum, trundling behind her a shopping basket on wheels: her dad swinging the RAF holdall that would contain his daily purchase of beer. He'd promised Mum no more of the hard stuff, just beer from now on. He marched as if he was traversing a parade-ground.

One morning, in the sad autumnal gloom of their spartan bedroom, Ilse saw Freddie writhing in agony.

'Freddie, oh Freddie, what's wrong?'

His face was too contorted, the pain too blinding for speech.

'I'll call the doctor.' She fled down the hall. Oh no, it was Sunday. Words blocked in her throat as she silently pleaded for someone to answer. Laboriously her call was transferred to an emergency number. The bedroom door opened. Freddie had dragged himself to the door-handle.

'Ilse, I'm all right. Don't worry.' Then his legs gave out and he fell to the floor.

'Come on,' screamed Ilse down the phone.

'Can I help you?' said a calm male voice.

'Come quickly. My husband's in terrible pain. Please, please come.'

'May I take your address? I'm coming now.'

She lay down next to her husband, cradling his head, laying her face next to his.

'They're coming, darling. It won't be long now. The pain will be gone.' His face was white and pinched. Did he hear her? His eyes were closed. On, where was the Freddie with the joke, the smile? Freddie. Why hadn't she noticed how thin he was? They'd both had a severe cold virus and lost weight, but hers had gone back on. Oh, why hadn't she noticed?

The doorbell rang. The young track-suited doctor came in. He examined Freddie.

'The ambulance is coming,' he said over his shoulder. He looked at her. His eyes talked, as if he knew things she did not. Yet.

So gently, as if wrapping a newly born baby, two enormous men covered Freddie in a white cellular blanket. They talked soothingly, and without causing him to shout with pain, they settled him into a mobile chair. They behaved casually, as if it was their tea-break. Numb, Ilse watched as the quartet went down the path to the gate. The early morning gale tore at his blanket. The doorbell, two men, the empty dawn – it was like the vivid description Michelle gave her of the secret police spiriting away her Onkel Felix.

The gate banged shut behind her. In her car she followed the ambulance through the deserted streets.

At the hospital casualty section she watched as they took off Freddie's pyjamas, dressing him instead in a smock. At last the tears came as she saw what had once been a body. The reassuring ambulance men hovered around the doorway. So used to buying and bartering, she gave them money as if it could buy deliverance from this place and she and Freddie could be back at their bungalow preparing for their early morning swim in the sea.

High up, a small window was lashed by rain, as she sat alone in a corridor, watching two people in white coats examining an X-ray. Zipped to the neck in one of her daughter's old track-suits, she waited with the same resignation as in the wartime queues; knowing that there might be nothing at the end of it.

'Ilse.' She followed the frail voice around the corner until she found Freddie, abandoned on a mobile stretcher in a dark corner. Quickly she snatched sun-glasses from her bag, so he wouldn't see her tears.

'I won't be long,' she said, before going off to find someone.

'How can you leave my husband all alone,' she shouted angrily at the first official medical person she saw.

'What are you going to do?'

'I'll get someone,' said the man irritably. The anger made no difference. It eased nothing. Slowly, she walked back to Freddie. They don't understand. Nobody knows. He brought me from nothing. I owe him everything and now he lies there and nobody takes any notice. Nobody cares.

It was a long trek through the darkest of valleys. The mountains that rose on either side each had a different label. Hospital. Radiotherapy. Doctor. Improvement. Deterioration. Hope. Despair.

'I see as usual, Daddy, you've charmed a posse of nurses. What do you do to make everyone fall in love with you?' said Mary, sitting easily on the edge of Freddie's bed.

'The same thing you do to young men, my dear.'

'Pity they're not more like you. Where can I find the recipe?'

'You're a very naughty girl and you'll go far. Not too far, I hope,' he chuckled, handing her the untouched grapes.

A weekly pattern was established. Ilse visited each afternoon, bringing fresh laundry and staying until his bedtime. Mary came at weekends.

'I can hear the sea,' he whispered, his hand, suntanned from their summer in the garden, lying in Ilse's.

'It's soothing, isn't it?' She turned the fan up higher so it would sound even more like the sea.

'What do they say?' he asked, looking straight into her eyes.

'I've talked with the doctor – a young woman with a streaming cold who told me all about her symptoms first,' laughed Ilse. 'She says she doesn't think you'll make ninety.'

'Oh well, that's all right then. I don't want to. What do you do in the mornings?'

'I keep your garden tidy so you won't have too much to do when you come home.'

The menu arrived and they went through the daily ritual of discussing choices even though he could only eat ice-cream.

One afternoon she climbed the stone stairway of the high-rise hospital annex. As she walked slowly down the familiar corridor, nurses rushed unseeingly by, disappearing into dreary ante-rooms, mud-yellow double doors clanging forlornly behind them. She could now see him through the doorway that led to his small windowless room. He sat with his hair on end as if each strand had been shot through with a steel spike. The only parts of him not covered by red blotches were his staring eyes. Bedclothes were strewn on the floor all around his mobile bed, which looked as though it had shot in at great speed. He was alone and uncomforted. A nearby basin lay upturned.

'Ilse.' Peace crept over his face, relaxing the muscles, sweetening the smile. 'Ilse.'

She resisted the urge to burst out 'Freddie, what's wrong? What have they done?' Instead she took his hand.

'Wait there. I'll be back in a moment.'

She found the consultant. Surely there was fear in his face when he saw her. This was the woman who always asked too many questions. Inconveniently she sought truth.

'There's been a reaction to the treatment,' he said to his pile of papers on the desk. How she hated his conservative grey suit, his pink bow-tie and his drumming fingers.

'Yes?'

'I think I know what it is.' He shrugged his shoulders as if their conversation was pointless.

Ilse turned her back on him and walked out. He followed her.

'Mrs Wheeler, please come back.'

Silently she allowed the pompous man to sit her down.

'We'll have to discontinue treatment,' he said more gently. 'We'll put him on heroin. There'll be no pain.'

'How long?' said Ilse, looking at the out-of-date calendar on the wall.

'Days. Weeks.'

'Do I tell him?'

The consultant's expression looked as if he had never been asked this question before. She didn't wait for an answer. The day's case history left him fiddling with his pink bow-tie.

In the late of the evening they moved Freddie to the ground floor next to the night-nurse station. Like a premature funeral procession, Ilse, two orderlies and the bed moved through subterranean passageways. The men were careless and bumped the bed against the lift doors. Freddie groaned. Ilse, anger spent, held his hand.

'It's all right, Freddie. We're nearly there. You'll be better soon.'

'Where are they taking me, Ilse?'

'Somewhere nice, *Liebling*. Somewhere nice.' They passed parts the general public were not meant to see. They went through hell to heaven as they came to rest in a carpeted room with flowers, wall paintings and maternal nurses who lifted him gently, bathed his sores and spoke in low voices.

Freddie, seeming to sense it was night, asked in agitation, 'Why are you here so late? Am I dying?'

'It's not late at all,' said Ilse untruthfully.

His eyes closed as he rested. She stroked his forehead, sometimes kissing it. She touched reverently the veins showing starkly in his hands. An essence rose from his forehead and beautiful in its gentleness evaporated into the air. She crept into bed next to him and curled up as close as possible. Later, a night nurse and her colleague covered Freddie and Ilse with a single blanket and turned down the light.

Unmuffled now by the cocoon of the hospital walls, she could hear the heave and sigh of the incoming tide. Nobody took any notice of the thin middle-aged woman sitting on the bench by the bus-stop. At her feet were two yellow bin bags.

BOOK IV

26

Dearest Renate,
Forgive me please. You kept writing and I did nothing, apart from Christmas cards. I just couldn't write about it. I didn't handle things very well at all. You'd think we'd get used to it. Time is supposed to heal. It doesn't. We just think of it less often. Other times we bury it away from public view. In confronting what you are going through, people are also looking into the crystal ball at what could happen to them. It is easier not to confront. You look the same to others and yet you feel as though you're dragging behind you a leg that won't work. Surely they must be able to see the wounds?

You'd think the first year would be the worst. It isn't, though. There's too much to reorganize. It hits you in the second year when the dust has settled and people have forgotten you're bereaved and can't think why you sometimes behave oddly. The body is in shock for a long time. One wonders how many times one can keep coming back.

I even let Freddie's lovely garden go to jungle. At last Mary could bear it no longer. She didn't say anything to me, just went out there and cleared the wilderness. I've never gardened, but one day I went out to help her. Thereafter we worked out there for hours, silently. Suffering drove us apart, gardening brought us together. You remember, Renate, you were always quoting from one of your favourite authors, a German doctor who had a nervous breakdown. For your healing, he said, go back to nature...

Whilst writing the difficult, long-overdue letter to her friend, Ilse was sitting on the deck-chair brought from their Petersham cottage of long ago. It was still stained with damp, but in constant use. In the vegetable patch next to her, fresh lettuce leaves had sprouted. Stiff-kneed, she eased herself up. Walking down the path to the house, she stumbled a little as she ducked to avoid an apple branch. One of her eyes wasn't too good and she didn't always see things in time. She'd inherited Vati's eyesight, of course. From the top of the oak wardrobe in her bedroom she hauled down a suitcase. Reverently she snapped the catches and parted the tissue paper. As she touched the material of the green coat, memories flooded back. It was a long time before she went out again into the garden to finish her letter.

...Renate, about the letter you have received via Heimstadt. I did know a Hans Bergermeister. He helped us escape from Liga to the west. The last I heard he had gone to a bridge-building site just outside Heimstadt. I never heard whether he married or not, but please do feel free to give his wife my address and an invitation to call on me when she is in

England. It's no distance at all from London to the south coast and I'm always in during the afternoon. I always wondered what happened to Hans. He was so kind. I would love to have met him again. So many disappeared after the war.

Oh Renate and to think you were there. You hid that revolutionary streak so well. I hope with all my heart that it happens although it is too late for me. Maybe I can manage a final trip east. As I sit here writing I can almost feel the pressure of the people . . . Mutti is so frail after her stroke and I am so far away, but I ought to be here as Mary always comes home at weekends. What is one to do? Always the tug at the heart-strings. I never imagined giving up one's nationality – even for love – would hurt so. It's as though one is always the outsider looking in through the pane of glass. I love the British. It's my fault that I never shake off the refugee feeling . . .

As the long, grey November day crawled into afternoon, the drizzle found entry into every crevice. The dampness played host to green algae. Cloth in hand, Ilse considered whether to make a start on cleaning the wall of the conservatory. The doorbell rang. Ilse peeped through the slats of the venetian blinds. A black London taxi was parked outside the gates. A neighbour was flicking out a duster. Her face disappeared quickly as if not wishing to seem curious about the elderly grey-haired woman with the battered luggage who now stood on Mrs Wheeler's doorstep. When Ilse opened the door she saw no elderly woman, only a vibrant flame-haired beauty with a medical bag at her side.

A blackbird was bursting its chest with song in the lilac tree, which was white when in bloom. The breeze in the tree-tops hushed as they put their arms around each other and wept.

'Michelle.' Decades were lifted away. The waterfall of emotion, frozen like stalactites, cascaded again. How had she lived all these years without sight of that face? 'Have you eaten?'

'Always we talk of food,' laughed Michelle; that same self-mocking sound. Memories of nurturing arms in a forest crawling with soldiers flowed through her.

In the deep cosiness that a settee in front of a coal fire and a tea-trolley set with buttered crumpets and teapot bring, when autumn furies rage outside the window, for Ilse and Michelle the past burned more vividly than the fire.

'It makes you believe in miracles, doesn't it? The long lonely years and now this, and we're both alive! I can't believe it.' Michelle's teacup rattled as her burn-marked hand set it down.

'Michelle, I searched everywhere for you. I pinched an RAF uniform so that I could have more freedom of movement. I don't know how many times I've written to the Missing Persons Inquiry office. So *you* were who Renate was telling me about!'

'Bergermeister. Yes.' smiled Michelle, biting into one of the crumpets. She ate slowly as so many of the grinding teeth were missing.

'I should have thought. I searched for you under the name of Weidel, and then when Renate wrote I still didn't work it out. I must be thick. Oh Michelle, why, why didn't you contact me? We've lost all those years.'

'I did contact you – at Heimstadt. When Germans were allowed to telephone again I got through. There were so few lines to the west and ordinary people weren't allowed to use them. Not where I was, anyway. A place where they put people they'd rather forget about.'

'No?'

'Yes. I'll tell you more later. Ernst became mayor of Liga, and he telephoned for me. The camp where you were is now a barracks for soldiers stationed out there under NATO. Renate, as you know, had gone. They were able to trace records of staff who had worked there, but they just said you'd gone to England. I figured you'd married the boss. It sounded, anyway, very much as if you were building a new life. A lot of people didn't want to broadcast the fact they were German at such a sensitive time. Me popping up from your past was what I didn't want for you.'

'Oh, how could you? I've missed you. There's always been heartache. I didn't know you weren't dead. How *could* you?'

'But what could we have done? The iron curtain came down and that was it. Me on one side, you on the other.'

'But before the Wall I came east several times alone to visit Mutti. And you were nearby. Why,' wailed Ilse, 'didn't you contact Mutti?'

'How could I? I was shut away for years, and when I came out I had nothing. It would have looked like begging. I had a nervous breakdown, and the hospitals were overflowing. Where could they put someone suffering from shock who had no family and no money? A mental institution.'

Ilse reached to touch her arm. It was at times like these, when emotions were too much for words that you wondered how such things could be allowed to happen.

As if reading her thoughts, Michelle asked, 'Do you

sometimes think that God doesn't usually give us what we *want*, but he gives us in the nick of time what we *need*?' Someone else, a long time ago had said those same words to Ilse.

'More often I don't know what I think any more. The older I get the more of a mystery the world seems,' sighed Ilse.

'One day the front door of the home was open. I could see an old white-haired man unloading some boxes. They say criminals can't disguise their back view and the way they walk. There was something so familiar about him. Then I remember thinking how all the men working were old. All the young men were dead.'

'We're the generation of manless women,' said Ilse wryly.

'The next minute I was out there, standing right next to him. "Michelle," he said straight away. 'How on earth could he have known me? I was an old crone and one of the inmates. "Michelle". He kept saying it over and over. Then a steely look came into his eyes. "Get in," he said, nodding to the open back doors of the van. "I can't, Hans, they'll find me – or the Stasi will. Visit me, please." I didn't want him to leave me, but I knew he'd come back. You know people who you've grown up with and played in the streets with as a child. I just knew he wouldn't leave me there.

Every Thursday I'd make sure I was somewhere in the neighbourhood of that front door. Each time we met our stories unfolded a little more. I thought "I want to take you away from all this" only happened in story-books, but eventually that's what happened. Hans and I married, Ernst did some string-pulling and got us a rented flat.'

Ilse disappeared into the kitchen to boil some more water. The teapot had gone cold, its temperature recording, like sand in an hourglass, the passage of time as they drew back the veil and looked down the years. She came back.

'Hans went back to the old town then?'

'When the bridge was built his job finished. There comes a time, I think – don't you? – when you want to return to roots, your own tribe.'

'Your own tribe,' said Ilse, wistfully.

'He had dreams of starting the family coffee business again. He got the factory site back but, as we saw, it was a heap of rubble. He hadn't the capital or, for that matter, the motivation. You need someone to graft for and all his family were dead. Also his lungs were in a terrible condition from all the building dust. He got a job working for another coffee merchant.'

The evening finally closed down – much earlier than usual. Ilse wriggled herself to the front of the settee so she could more easily use her arms to lever herself up. She switched on the table lamps, which made warm yellow pools of light in various parts of the room, and drew together the brown velvet curtains, shutting out the night. Michelle watched. They smiled at each other in quiet happiness.

'Safe now,' said Ilse. She went into the kitchen to make hot drinks, calling 'Don't you dare move. You've done all the travelling today. I'm doing the rest.'

She came back into the room, a hot-water bottle under her arm. Gathering up Michelle's luggage, she disappeared into a room, from which came sounds of intense activity.

Later, with her friend snugly propped against multiple pillows and sipping a drink, Ilse again fetched the shabby suitcase. Intrigued, Michelle watched every move, wrinkling her nose unconsciously as the strong smell of moth-balls rose.

'Oh Ilse,' she breathed, 'and to think what we've got that coat to thank for. Although considering where I ended up, you'd hardly call my interview successful.'

Ilse sat on the edge of the bed, distractedly fingering the coat's material. Suddenly she laughed.

'I've got a very nosy neighbour on that side. She's always shaking her duster out when my doorbell rings. I can see her face now if we told her the half of what we've done. It'd surely lower her property value if it were known she lived next door to a shop-lifter.' She laughed again, then it trailed away as she saw herself surging down that desolate street, hemmed in by a mob of looters. It can't have been her. Starving, but all that fire, all that energy, all that youth. Where did it all go? She came back to find Michelle looking at her.

'You were a long way away. Where were you?'

'Looting. Just a bit of looting. You're worn out. We'll talk in the morning.' Tenderly, she kissed her forehead and closed the door softly behind her.

When she looked in again, Michelle was sleeping. Her finger was still curled around the mug handle. Without waking the sleeper, she prised it from her. The fingers wore no rings, and the texture of the skin was rough from a lifetime's work – instruments that had ministered comfort to so many. Thousands owed their lives to the expertise of these hands. Some might even be thinking of her now, talking about her, wondering where she was, if she was alive. And here she was in Ilse's home tonight. The knuckles rested against the white of the counterpane. They were swollen as if arthritis was robbing them. The nails of the slender fingers were clean and short, and though asleep throbbed with life, so unlike the porcelain brittleness of Freddie's at the end.

The rain had eased off. Ilse felt restless. As she walked

under the dripping fruit-tree branches, half a moon appeared briefly. Like a laser, it penetrated the garden with a strange light. She could not look. A train rumbled over the nearby crossing. Quickly she slipped into the summer-house and switched on the light. She uncovered her easel, then settled herself on the pink rush bedroom seat at the far end. One leg draped over the arm of the chair, she stared for a long time at the half-completed oil-painting – a young woman in flight against a wall of fire. So long ago. Did it all ever really happen? It must have. There were the scars on Michelle's hands and the green coat. Funny she'd never worn green since. Perhaps for the same reason Freddie wouldn't touch the sort of food he had to eat in his student days because it was a reminder of when he had nothing.

'Oh, I do wish it was summer and we could have tea in the garden. Mary's trained wild roses – those with the delicate pale yellow – and Dorothy Perkins up the patio walls.'

'Is she like Freddie?'

'Same temperament but not like either of us in looks. I know what. . . .' Ilse stopped, realizing again that there were huge areas of each other's lives neither knew about.'

'Go on,' said Michelle, sipping from the Liga bone-china teacup, one of a set which had arrived unbroken from Mutti some years ago.

'Birgit was the office problem. No, that's unfair. After all, she gave me a job. Had she decided she didn't want me, I'm sure at that time Freddie would have been influenced by her. She was a bit . . . um . . . bossy.'

'You were just about to tell me what Birgit would have said about Mary not looking like either you or Freddie.'

'She liked to stir things. I think most offices survive the boredom by regular bits of scandal. It's marvellous as long as it's not about you. She wanted Freddie badly, so as you can imagine she was not favourably disposed towards me. She married the wheeler-dealer, Reggie. He could get anything – at a price. He scared me. I always wondered exactly what the price would be and when the paying would stop if you allowed him to get a hold over you. He seemed to be completely moral-less – if there is such a word. He spotted Freddie and me meeting on trains before the fraternization ban had been lifted.'

'Somehow I never imagined you married. You seemed destined for a career.'

'Life seems to have its own ideas for us. Freddie wasn't a man you could easily say no to. I did call it off once, and he went in for a spate of bar wrecking. He was the sort of person that filled a room, and when he left it was as though someone had switched the sun off. And yet between all the good times, we often made each other pretty miserable. I couldn't stand his drinking and he couldn't stand my long silences. I wonder sometimes if it is ever possible to live in harmony with another human being.'

They sat quietly.

'Now tell me; what happened?'

Michelle knew exactly what Ilse meant by this.

'That's been the hell, that I went there to help. I could have helped and I didn't. I can't ever forget the last picture. I think it was the women's quarters we went into first. A woman stretched out her hand to me. The only part that lived were her luminous eyes – eyes like yours, Ilse. Then she died. The joy of liberation was too much. I passed out. I don't know where they took me but when I came to I couldn't go on. We'd been malnourished for years, hadn't we? But it's no excuse. I went there to help and I was useless. I didn't even manage to tell them where I was from. They worked it out from the name of the Liga leathermakers inside my case.'

The letter-box clattered as the newspapers arrived. Michelle's head was bowed.

'We should have lived off my job, as I wanted,' Ilse told her. 'You were too weak to help but you wouldn't budge.'

'Then I'd have had to live with the fact that I didn't use my skills to help them.'

'You've no right to torture yourself. You've done so much for others. I've seen you. When you're doing your job you give everything, as if each patient is as vulnerable and important as a newly born baby. You've rarely considered your own needs. Isn't it about time you learned to take?'

Ilse went to get another coffee for her friend. Having lived through the era of substitute foods, she could never stop wallowing in the luxurious scent of fresh coffee beans. The foul brew that had passed for coffee, delightfully nicknamed Muckefuck by the forces, was not a part of the past she hankered after. Whilst in the kitchen, she jotted down some items on the shopping list. Mary would be joining them at the weekend.

Back in the sitting room, arms folded, and staring out through the glassed-in porch to the front garden, Ilse let her thoughts flick to the future. It was a rare occasion.

'We know so much. I thought I could pass on my experience to Mary, but she doesn't want to know. Perhaps she's wiser than I am when she says "Mum, I've got to learn from my own mistakes." Maybe, Michelle, our generation's time has gone and we pass the baton on to those who are fitter and faster and younger. How do we stop them making the same mistakes?'

'We've still got things to do. I've got a couple of interesting cards up my sleeve which I want to play and see what happens. The old female curiosity bit again.'

'Ooh Michelle, what?' Ilse put on a show of a small girl being excited.

'You'll have to let me stay a little longer if you want to know,' teased Michelle.

'I don't ever want to let you out of my sight again.'

27

The fence wobbled a little as the gate banged.
'Mum.'
A door slammed.
The sunny front porch filled with energy. Sunlight danced on Michelle's spectacles, transforming them into two rings of coloured fire. She put aside the newspaper which she had been scanning for snippets of news of Germany. The fair-haired young-looking woman loaded down with books stopped. Realizing she had been standing with her mouth open, she quickly put the books onto the table by the fireplace.

Eyebrows raised in question marks, she said, 'Good morning.' Her mother never had visitors. Who could it be, this elderly woman with the kind face and damaged hand?

Michelle eased herself stiff-jointedly from the armchair.

'Hello, I'm Michelle, a friend of your mother's.'
Still mystified, Mary asked, 'From Liga?'
'Yes from Liga.'
'Liga. Mum's often talked about it.'
Michelle noticed the young woman hadn't said 'Mum's often talked about you.' Feeling the silence had gone on rather too long she broke it by saying, 'Il—your mother's in the garden.'

'Thank you,' she said politely, brushing past and

making for the back door.

The sitting-room, which spanned the full width of the bungalow, had large windows at each end. Through the back one, Michelle had a view of the summer-house and the entire back garden. Ilse emerged from her morning's painting at the second call of 'Mum'. The daughter kissed her mother on the cheek. There was a lot of hand-waving as they talked. Mary seemed to be telling her off, then she took her mother's arm as they walked down the path. Michelle didn't miss the look of pain on Mary's face when Ilse shook off the assistance.

'You've met Mary,' said Ilse unnecessarily when they came into the house.

'Yes,' said Michelle, rather quietly.

'It's lovely to have a guest,' said Mary brightly, as if making amends for her earlier lukewarm welcome.

'Thank you. Just a short visit.' Michelle wanted to reassure the young woman that she wasn't going to be stuck with some old biddy for an indefinite length of time, but Ilse looked upset and turned away.

'*Erbsen*, Mrs Bergermeister?' asked Mary, flicking back a strand of long hair and juggling with the dish of peas. There seemed no household rule of thumb as to when one language was used and when the other.

'Thank you,' said Michelle with equal politeness.

Ilse pushed a potato uneasily around her plate. She didn't look at either of them. It wasn't how she'd imagined things. Mary had never pressed her for stories about the war because she knew how quickly they upset her. She heard her mother's nightmares – harrowing scenes when she imagined Gestapo arms pinioned her – sat with her during thunderstorms, never knowing why they reduced her mother to a quivering wreck. Keeping silent about so much was Ilse's method of emotional survival. This late in her life she was learning she risked alienating those she loved. By keeping her thoughts and memories secret, she must make them feel she was not trusting them. Did they really feel excluded and unneeded? If only they knew how much she needed them. She tried to be so strong in order to cover up how weak and afraid she felt most of the time.

'More meat Lieb . . . uh, Ilse?'

'No thank you.' As she waved away the unwanted dish, she knocked over her wineglass. The red liquid soaked like blood into the crisp linen white of the table-cloth. Mary's dive for the kitchen and subsequent mopping-up brought relief from the tension.

'No problem,' said Mary, ducking under the oak dining-table to staunch the gathering pool on the floor.

'Thanks, darling. I seem to get clumsier as I get older,' said a confused Ilse. Oh, the isolation! She felt so cut off from these two. Something was wrong with her body and she couldn't pin-point what it was. She felt as though she could see her loved ones only through the bottom of a glass. They were visible but distorted and so separate. Depression's possessive fingers were tightened around her throat. When you are young and a love affair goes wrong, you can long romantically for death. When old, the reality of death can seem more palatable than waiting for the painful end to the story.

'There are usually some people I know at the sailing club at this time. Is it OK, Mum, if I pile the pots in the sink and do them later?' Michelle smiled.

'You go now, Mary. We'll do them.'

After Mary had gone and they were settled in the rocking-chair and armchair either side of the fireplace, Michelle said rather sternly, 'Don't even think about washing up now. We've got important things to discuss. Enough of this British reserve. What is wrong, Ilse? Talk to me. Why didn't you tell Mary about me?'

Ilse studied her hands. Her face rarely held expression apart from a resigned sadness.

'There were a lot of things I got out of the habit of talking about. When I first came to this country I was more outgoing. I talked about the bombing and what it had done to ordinary people. I'd hardly ever finish an explanation before they'd say "Look what you did to our cities." Eventually I buried the past. I thought, "Let Mary make a fresh start." She shouldn't be saddled with being the daughter of that German woman. She survived Liga, you know, etc. I think Mary assumed Renate – my pen-friend, the one you wrote to – was you. You were something too special to mention. I didn't want it trampled over by ordinary life. It felt as if talking about it would burst the bubble. Thoughts of you because my life-raft through troubled times. Oh Michelle, please, you're not on a short visit, are you?'

'I'm here for as long as you want me, but let's talk about that another time. Look, the sun's shining. Let's walk down to the sea.'

Sobered up from the adrenalin high of the blowy seafront walk, they grew rather maudlin over tea.

'It's too late for us, isn't it? You know, Freddie never met them,' said Ilse, looking at the wall photo of her parents. 'Mutti's so frail. The matron has to write for her since her stroke.'

'How long since you've been?'

'Not since the wall went up. Decades. Not since Mary got German measles. She was with Freddie at the circus and felt faint. Freddie was so good with her. He'd taken his holiday just so he could stay home and look after her whilst I visited Mutti. When I got back he'd decorated the dining-room.'

Michelle fiddled with her watch-strap whilst she mulled over this information.

'You know, my mind's like a little bird on a twig. It flits from branch to branch, never staying long in one place. I have to really work at concentrating. Key words that you use spark off a train of thought and then I find I'm not listening to you properly. Shout at me, Ilse, when that happens.'

'Well, you know what they say. It's downhill all the way from twenty, and you were pretty old when I met you.'

'Cheeky cow,' laughed Michelle. 'I was thinking, though, do you think there's any such thing as co-incidence? Do we meet people again just by chance, or do we meet them because we have willed it? Wouldn't it be a beautiful thought if we were all locked into some gigantic telepathic network. If we discover this infra-structure, do you think it will spawn a whole new breed of telepathic engineers?'

'What a lovely idea. Tell me more of Hans. How much warmth that man could put into one word! Every human being should have a big brother like him. There'd be more secure people walking around if we got that lucky.'

'As I said, he got a job delivering coffee and various other things. Just when it seemed I had no future but more of the same, the *liebe Gott* decides he'll send someone to watch over me. It makes you want to believe, doesn't it?

'One accepts that marriage is the consummation of passionate feeling, but we had a quiet survival kind of friendship. Perhaps it was the more enduring; I don't know. I know there were no expectations on either side, just an acknowledgement that in hard times two heads are better than one. But it was good. I'm a lucky woman. I was able to nurse him when he got too ill to work. As you know, he always was bronchial. Oh Ilse, his lungs were clapped out from building dust and overwork. He wasn't cut out for manual labour. We both know what it did to those who aren't. Racehorses and cart-horses, I remember Ernst telling me.

'It was pneumonia took him off in the end, one Saturday in November. It was warm for the time of year and there was a light rain like a spray. The window was open and the curtain moved as if waving. A single bed in a single room. The sweetness of his smile and his last words.

' "Michelle, it hurts here." Then he went. Such a huge man. Surely they can't die like the rest of us? He looked so small then. There was such gentleness in the passing the grieving was bearable. It was time. Nature usually knows. I'm always thankful he was spared more pain, and when terrible things happen in the world I say to myself, "They can't hurt you now, Hans." ' Michelle said it all so calmly, as if telling her friend what she had bought at the shops the other day.

Ilse blew her nose on a tissue. 'Your mother, our escape, your illness – he always appeared when you needed help. Perhaps you're ahead of your time with this telepathy theory. I feel privileged to have known Hans. If anyone asked for help, he gave it. He behaved as if you were doing him a favour.'

Half a sun still struggled over the summer-house roof, its last rays sneaking into the darkening sitting-room. It sank fast until they were left with the glow of the electric fire.

'Karl?'

'All I know is he married a local girl from Heimstadt

and stayed there. Ernst and Hans felt the urge to get back to their roots. Ernst worked in local government – as I told you, he rose to mayor – and he wanted a say in how Liga was rebuilt. Fat chance. He was a puppet. The state authorities pulled his strings.'

It was the time of day when energy ebbed. Michelle went to her room, whilst Ilse wandered down the garden. She was restless. Changes were in the air. She felt racked by uncertainty. Why? Everything was so good now. She should feel complete.

Since lunchtime the wind had dropped. Yet when she asked, 'Where now, Vati?' the ivy on the wall lifted as air tunnelled under it. Its leaves flared, showing pale underbellies. With a sigh and a sob it lay back flat on the flint wall.

'I've been so wrong about so many things. I wish I had known what I know now when you were alive. How we could have talked.'

Mary came in late. The two women had gone to bed. The telephone was in the hall, and it was difficult to avoid overhearing conversations. There was the sound of buttons being pressed, a slight squeak after each digit.

'Hello, it's me.'
'Oh, fine, you know.'
'Mum has a guest.'
'Amazing.'
'We're going there.'
'Why do you think.'
'Because it's a life experience, and now the Wall's come down, why not? . . .'
'Well, we don't see things in quite the same way, do we?'
'Suit yourself.'
A phone was banged down. The day ended.

28

'I'm all right, dear. You make sure your mum doesn't get lost,' said Michelle calmly to Mary, who was kneeling by her feet, holding a wad of tissues to stem the blood that was flowing from her knee through the gash in her tights. 'Ilse does fuss sometimes.'

Michelle had fallen against one of the airport's wire luggage trolleys, opening up her knee on one of its sharp metal edges. Ilse was searching out a first-aid post.

'Are *you* all right?' asked Michelle. The young woman's face was so white and tense. She went on, 'It's not easy having strangers in your home.'

'I like having you stay. You're so good for Mum. She never talks, you know. Just bottles things up.'

'Look who's talking.' They both laughed.

'Well, it's . . . no, it's OK.'

'Enough of my leg. It's all right, thank you. I'm a tough old bird. I should be by now. Go on.'

'It's Mike.' Mary burst out. 'He wants to get engaged. He's been doing the same course as me. I like him a lot. He's funny and a friend, but I've just started a new course – a bit late in life, I know, to add some more qualifications – but it means I work all day and study in the evenings, and I'm not sure I'm the marrying type. I don't know what to do. Because I can't make my mind up, he thinks I don't love him, and we're fighting all the time now. It used to be so good.'

Michelle didn't rush into a response. She just sighed and watched a young mother trying to control two small children whilst waiting for her luggage to come through on the conveyor belt. At last there was the quick report of a smack. Richly deserved, but others looked on in disapproval.

'There aren't any answers. Everyone's life is unique. What's good for one makes someone else miserable. I think when you know someone is right, and the time is right, you won't be talking to me like this. You'll just do it. Like your mother did with your father. All her worldly goods in one suitcase and off she went to a strange country.'

'But how do you know if you love someone?'

'The world's greatest philosophers haven't worked that one out yet. Love. What is it? Something that can't be seen or bought on a street corner. You can't search for it. You can't see it. It demands everything you've got, and that still isn't enough. You do things for someone because you wouldn't dream of not meeting their needs. You're there for them when they are suffering, even though they hardly notice you and take you for granted. When they're bereaved you listen for hours because you know they need to talk about the person who's died. It's taking them to the doctor when they feel ill. It's doing things for them without the expectation of rewards like appreciation, money or sex. The other simply flows through your veins.'

Mary wrapped the blood-stained tissue in newspaper.

'That's beautiful.'

'Build your career. It's important, it's part of who you are. If you love your work you have everything. The other will come to you – when you're ready. Maybe now isn't the right time for you to take someone into your life.'

At last their train drew into the land of monstrous chimneys, belching smoke and dingy apartment blocks. Hundreds of pylons stole the once-Gothic skyline from the church steeples. Acre after acre of industrial graveyards were filled with goods trucks that idled and rusted into the oil-drenched earth. Back to the land of their youth; a black cavern in the east, bled dry of machines and now of people.

Slowing and squealing, the train came to rest in Liga Station. Michelle gave an involuntary gasp at the sight of a group of men working on an adjacent line. Mary observed silence, busying herself with reaching for their bags and setting them two by two on the compartment floor. Ilse sat immobile, as impassive as always.

Though in the early years she had returned to the east since becoming a British national, she had always travelled alone. This visit was heart-warmingly different. Previously her loyalties had been cruelly divided: her mother behind the Wall, her husband and child back home. Funny she thought 'home' was where her family was and not the country of her birth. But today was so different.

'Both my loved ones with me,' she said, linking arms with them. Michelle squeezed her hand. Mary gazed around at the scene of her mother's sketchy stories. Ilse looked up to the rafters where the offices had been. Their stone patterns with gargoyles and mullioned windows had not been replaced. Instead there were concrete blocks and huge areas of sheet glass. Vati's gold-rimmed spectacles did not glint down at her. There was no wave. No colleagues called to her, 'Thank goodness you've come, Ilse. At least you're not squeamish. We've kept the unprettiest job for you.' There was no Frau Reinhardt goading her with the word 'chicken'.

Ilse glanced at her watch. It was the time of day when people were homeward-bound after a day's excursion or going out for the evening, but the scene was deserted save for a partial view of a seated woman who was obviously in charge of the ladies' loo. Michelle headed for the newspaper stand, whilst Mary disappeared in the direction of the cloakroom. Ilse stood alone in the vast amphitheatre. She had only ever known it throbbing with people. Even when she did nights there was a constant turnover of travellers as the trains ran all night and one felt at the very pulse of the communications network. This emptiness was eerie. She wished Frau Reinhardt would march from her lair behind those opaque-glassed doors and tick her off. Mary's laughter brought her out of her trance.

'Well I must say, Mum, the entrepreneurial spirit is alive and kicking in Liga. I thought "spend a penny" went out with the ark but here you spend eighty pfennigs. When she heard my German spoken in an English accent and I gave her a ten-mark note she cottoned on to the fact I might not understand the money and gave me twenty pfennigs change. I'd gone round the corner before I realized she owed me nine marks. She had it piled up in readiness but she wasn't going to give it to me unless I asked. Nice one. I wonder how many times it's worked?'

'I think she met her match in you, dear. You've never been behind the door,' smiled her mother. Whilst reading the front page of a newspaper Michelle wandered over.

'I see the firm where I used to do a spot of health visiting is relocating to Berlin. Right are we all set? We can walk. My flat's not far.'

'We can, but how about you?' said Ilse, looking down at Michelle's bandaged knee.

'Heavens, I'm all right. It's only a surface wound.' They turned down an alley-way that ran between the station wall and a boarded-up warehouse that had seen better times. Its stucco had fallen away to reveal bricks underneath. On the remaining patches of the old facade was faded lettering:

H Bergermeister GmbH

'Quick,' hissed Michelle and with a speed that made a mockery of her age and injury she started to run. Asking no questions they followed suit.

As there was only room for a single-file progress, they held their bags out in front of them, and like rats down a sewer pipe squirmed their way along the narrow passage. Mary brought up the rear, wondering if either of them was going to have a heart attack. This trip with the two old ducks was turning into quite an adventure.

'Come on,' urged Michelle over her shoulder. As they ran, their feet slithered on a gooey mixture of sodden newspapers. At last they came out into a street lined with low-rise flats, drab grey concrete structures far removed from velvet curtains and gardeners. Everywhere there was shuddering stillness.

'What was all that about?' heaved Ilse, setting down her bags and leaning against the wall surrounding a yard that held nothing but rusting washing posts.

'Football match. I remembered it was today when I heard them. It's coming-out time. If they lost, we might be in a bit of trouble. Don't worry, they won't come this way. They go down that road to the station.'

'Oh, hooligans. We've plenty of those in England.'

'Not like these, I hope,' said Michelle, picking up her bags. She glanced anxiously up and down the street before saying, 'It's getting nasty. Very political. Swastika tattoos, Molotov cocktails, baseball bats – that sort of thing. We keep our heads down when they're playing at home.' Again Michelle spoke matter-of-factly as though the conversation was about the weather.

'Are all these flats empty?' asked Mary.

'Many of them, yes. Only the old are left. The skilled young have gone west after jobs. Nobody's coming east, because there are less and less jobs. It looks as if we're going to have to start all over again; like after the war, when our savings were of no value and all we had was forty marks.' Michelle's steps became slower and shorter. They fell silent. Surely their bags had got heavier. Each road had the same five-storey boxes with open balconies, some of which were hung with washing. Not a head showed. The message from the dwellings could not have been more eloquent had they been daubed with graffiti saying 'We do not want to get involved.' The streets lay there, available to any marauding gang that wished to take possession of them.

'We're lucky, we'll be home before any of those who live round here get this far. Most of them are unemployed. They hang around the street corners all day. It's very frightening.'

'No taxis?' said Mary innocently.

'Too expensive,' replied Michelle. 'Unreliable too. The spare-parts factory closed down long ago, and the cars that are about are on their last gasp.'

The weary trio stopped outside a building with no distinguishing features. Here and there were punched eyelets of windows. Some were curtainless as if an eyelash was missing.

'Home.'

Ilse and Mary said nothing.

'We'll have to walk up. We don't have a lift.'

'Leave the bags here. You two go up in your own time. I'll bring the luggage up a floor at a time,' said Mary, taking charge of the legwork. Negotiating the fireproof stone steps two at a time, she sprang up to the first floor. Back she came for the next lot. Ilse took Michelle's arm. Heads bent in concentration, they completed a leisurely marathon to the fourth floor.

Michelle searched her coat pocket, drawing out a leather purse with curled-up edges. There was a tight feeling in Ilse's chest as she watched the fingers dealing with the keys. She remembered the smoke-blackened ones of long ago. One lock undone. Now a key for the second one – a heavy-duty security affair. The cumbersome door bumped sluggishly against the wall as though it cared little whether they came or went. A long dark hallway was revealed. It was ages since the walls had been painted. Charitably it could be called antique. The flat had a desolate air. 'My owner is away' it seemed to say. The door at the end of the corridor was open. It drew you down, an oasis after a bleak journey. Books were piled onto a table, and the painting of a child trying on her mother's shoes looked down on this cell of an intellectual.

'Industrial rape.' The artist in Ilse drew her to the view. She was heart-broken. This wasn't like the Liga landscapes stacked in her summer-house. 'I've never seen it from so high up. The cost, Michelle, the cost. This isn't worth what it's cost.'

'Come and sit down. Don't think about it,' said Michelle in a choked voice, seeing through Ilse's eyes what she took for granted. 'There is a future. I've seen to it.'

29

The home for those requiring full-time nursing care was, like everything else, nearing the point of dereliction. Hope fluttered only briefly when she met Frau Hoffman, a small squat woman with ginger hair that grew out grey. Her eyes were cool and a bit watchful as she shook hands with Ilse.

'Pleased to meet you, Frau Wheeler.'

'Thank you. How is my mother?'

'She's in the sitting-room. She's very weak, but we like them all to get up for some part of the day if possible. I'd like you to speak with the doctor first. He's my son. He calls here on his daily round. We're in his area.'

'Thank you, Frau Hoffman. May I introduce my friend and my daughter? I wonder, is there somewhere they could wait?'

The matron's frown was so brief before the features were rearranged that only Ilse noticed. How she hated the consummate actress types with their lack of spontaneity and humour.

'Here would be all right.' She indicated the row of cheap chairs outside her office door.

Feeling like a couple of gatecrashers, Michelle and Mary obediently sat down.

'If you'd like to come with me,' said the matron.

Ilse raised her eyebrows and mouthed to her support group, 'See you later.'

Dr Ottmar Hoffman had a close-fitting cap of jet-black hair, precision clipped like his moustache. Though young, his shoulders hunched with responsibility as he pored over papers on his desk. Funny. Visiting doctors didn't usually have an office on the premises. If it wasn't his office, he looked mighty at home in it. The eyes that looked up at Ilse were frighteningly intense. She would have ridiculed the expression that eyes could bore through you, but these did. Quickly he got to his feet and bowed his head in her direction.

'A seat please, Frau Wheeler. My apologies for the mess. We have no cleaners at present. We shall shortly be recruiting some.' There was a slight pause as they appraised each other. A young man of high ideals, possibly? How dangerous that could be.

'I understand it is a long time since you have seen your mother?'

It was only a statement, and made without the slightest hint of criticism, yet the guilt rose up in her. How to ration love? Who comes first? Mother, husband, child or friend? How much to each?

'No,' she replied, feeling the one word was not enough, but she really didn't wish to explain.

'Your mother recovered well from her stroke. Thankfully a minor one. You will, I'm afraid, notice some lapses of memory and confusion from time to time. Be prepared she may not recognize you.'

Rubbish, thought Ilse. What do you know? She didn't want to believe what he was saying. She nodded that she had received and understood the information. He stood up. She followed suit. His face wore a worried look as he opened the door for her. Unspeaking, he escorted her down a bulbless corridor. Ilse smiled grimly to herself. Story of her life. When she got to the other side they'd sure as hell have used up their last light bulb.

Like a puppy scenting its mother, Ilse rushed at the upright armchair, whose occupant was so frail, the wings of the chair almost hid her from view. Ilse never saw the roomful of inmates, some in bizarre shapes as they turned foetus-like to an inner world. She had no eyes for the care assistant who crouched by the side of the dribbling man as he ate. She saw only the woman who had been in charge of the kitchen, the chocolate box with the kitten, and her life.

'Mutti.' Gently she held her mother's hand in her own. 'Mutti.' The hair was so thin and totally white. Where the face used to go out, it sank in. She longed to hear her name from those soft lips. Mutti's eyes had the tiniest of black pupils, hardly there at all. They looked at her. Did they see her?

Dr Hoffman hovered. Mutti turned to him. 'My sister,' she said, pointing to Ilse.

'I'll leave you alone for a while,' said the doctor. Mutti gave her the sweetest of smiles and clung like a fallen nestling to her hand. Ilse knew her mother sensed she was someone special. Someone who belonged to her. Surely a parent knows its young? Just to hold hands was enough. This woman had given her life, struggled for her, and now when she needed her daughter most, Ilse could do so little.

'A chocolate, Mutti?'

Outside the door, Ilse leaned against the wall. Beaten-spirited, she looked one way, then the other. Corridors and more corridors, their green shiny linoleum of an unmemorable pattern. Leading where? To blank walls and more blank walls? She felt her body running down. Wherever she was going, she was sure she'd need either a train or a corridor to get her there. One lonely light bulb gleaming between here and the turning at the end. She and Michelle had seen death come often enough to know when its visit was near. The last buffer would be gone. She would be an orphan finally. When she was free to travel at last it was too late for Mutti. She straightened up, squared her shoulders, and strode purposefully back to matron's office. It wasn't too late for Michelle and Mary. It was time she gave a bit more.

They were still obediently installed on their chairs for all the world as if they were outside a headmistress's study, awaiting punishment. They looked up as if from a deep conversation. Ilse felt a twinge of envy at their comfort with each other. If only she could slough off this hair shirt of self-sufficiency.

'May we see her?' asked Michelle.

'She might not know you,' said Ilse, close to tears. 'But I'd like you to see her. Do you think one at a time would be better for her?'

'Which door, sweetie?' said Michelle, moist-eyed.

'Round the corner. Second on the left.' Ilse sat down, nearly missing the chair. Mary caught her just in time.

'Clumsy, Mum.'

'Yes, I must take more care.' What was happening to her? She hadn't seen the wineglass. She hadn't seen the chair. Next time it might be a bus. It was all right now. She could see the matron's desk, the notice-board, and the high window with dust clinging to it. She could also see Frau Hoffman bidding good-bye to two shaven-headed young men. They did not *feel* like relatives but she supposed they must be.

Washing up the breakfast things in the convenienceless kitchen that would have appalled a British housewife, Mary talked of her new crush.

'He's so gentle with them. He treats them like a piece

of priceless Meissen and never talks down to them even though they're so muddled.'

'His mother seems a pleasant enough woman,' said Ilse, putting the canister of dried milk away.

'That's what we said of neighbours who we later found had been informing on us for years,' muttered Michelle to the washing-up water.

'It's not like you to be so cynical,' said Ilse, surprised. She'd hardly known Michelle say anything bad about anyone.

'Sorry. A bad habit I've acquired. You never knew round these parts who you could trust. You ended up suspecting everybody.'

'Whilst I was visiting Grandma he got called away on an emergency,' added Mary.

'Oh?' asked Michelle curiously.

'A Vietnamese had been stabbed.'

'That figures.' They both looked at Michelle, who said nothing further apart from, 'I'm sure he's a nice young man.' Without reading anything into the expression on Michelle's face, Mary went off to the nursing home.

Over morning coffee, Ilse said, 'You've changed.'

'Not with you. Though faith gets defaced by mistrust and cynicism over the years. One becomes secretive. Every brick seems to have an ear. I have to learn all over again to be more open about how I feel.'

Ilse started to laugh. She had to put her coffee-cup down.

'And I thought that was my problem You've always been wonderwoman to me. Don't, after all these years show me you're mortal.'

Michelle started to laugh too.

'It's high time both of us stopped trying to be so

strong and marvellous all the time,' Ilse went on 'Look how many years we've lost, each thinking the other didn't need her. Because I'm younger than you, you still see me as tough and undefeated and full of go. I'm not. I'm old and slow and I don't see too well. I need glasses and a magnifying glass. I keep knocking things over, and I need you, and right now I could do with a hug.'

'What a couple of twits. I've a squalid flat and a meagre pension, but I can give you a hug.'

As if someone had turned up the volume on a radio, the baying of many human voices came from the street far below. The two friends peered cautiously from the window. The placards told the story. It was time to take to the streets again to beg the west to take notice that they were sinking into the quicksand of mass unemployment. This was the early warning that here was a fertile seed-bed in which disaster could bloom.

'The devil makes work for idle hands. Too late we find out how true the old sayings can be,' said Michelle, her arm around Ilse's shoulder. They were far above the action but felt no smugness or safety.

Back on the settee, Michelle said, 'I'm starting a job next week. Only part-time.'

'But Michelle, have you the strength now? Even part-time, seeing to the general public is very demanding.'

'Oh, it's not medical. Office cleaning.'

'Cleaning!'

'What's wrong with cleaning?'

'You're a qualified and skilled doctor, that's what's wrong.'

'Yes, a qualified and skilled doctor whose hands shake and who's spent time in a mental home. In a time of no jobs, I don't think my curriculum vitae will impress.'

'But Michelle, cleaning?'

'There's no "but" about it. I'm one of the lucky ones. I've found a job. Three-quarters of my monthly pension goes on heating, rent and health insurance. They tell me they're going to double my rent. I've no choice but to work. I'm just grateful I've found employment.'

By the time Mary came home it was beginning to get dark and the two women were edgy. She was lit up with the success of her mission. Hearing a rumour that a local butcher had taken delivery of some meat, she had joined the queue, and hadn't come away empty-handed.

'You look just like your mother when she came back from one of her foraging trips. Such pride as she unloaded her rucksack. We ate almost as she unpacked.'

Mary wasn't listening. 'He's got super eyes and he's so keen on the theatre. I did theatre design as my subsidiary at college. I think he may ask me out. He's awfully interested in England and asks a lot of questions. Funnily enough, about boring things like politics.'

'Does he now?' replied Michelle speculatively. 'A deep-thinking young man, by the sounds of things. It's a wonder he doesn't go for a better-paid job in the west.'

'He says he has a mission here,' enthused Mary.

'Funny he gets all the violence cases. Oh, by the way Ilse, I'll be out tomorrow morning. Got to see a man about a dog.'

30

Enveloped all the way in its own smoke cloud, the yellow Trabant coughed to a halt at the same tram-stop from which Ilse had fled home well over forty years ago. This far, all she had seen of the taxi-driver was the back of his greasy black cap from which ebullient clumps of grey hair escaped and his cheerful red and white neckerchief.

'This is about as far as the old tub will go. Won't make it up there I'm afraid, *gnädige Frau*,' he apologized, looking up at the steep path that led to the former Weinacht residence.

'Still a bit of life left in me, though. Allow me,' and he offered Michelle his arm.

'You're a kind man,' she said, walking slowly up the hill, using his arm as a support when the bad leg misbehaved.

'Doesn't look as if anyone's at home,' said the driver, scratching his head at the desolation. Still early in the year, morning frost trimmed every blade of the wilderness. It was years since the roses had been deadheaded. The path leading to the front door was humped with tussocks. The flagstone slabs were breaking up. Searing Eastern European winds had denuded the rotting dovecote of its paint. Many of the windows were boarded up, but one wing seemed occupied. Its windows, like eyes, looked out over Liga. If windows had souls, they would have wept.

'Someone does live here,' said Michelle.

'Look, *gnädige Frau*, rather than me waiting while you run up a big bill, why don't I do a couple of other calls and come back in an hour?'

'I'd appreciate that.' Michelle paid his fare so far. He waved away the offered tip.

Skirting the pot-holes, she walked round to the back door. Ilse must never see this. The smell was rancid. Even the cold air didn't purify it. Further up the slope a chemical factory emptied its debris into the skies. Behind a thin veil of bushes, workers' flats stretched to the horizon.

Her knock was answered by an older woman dressed in a floral-patterned button-up overall. This must be the new housekeeper.

'Sir is expecting you, Frau Bergermeister.'

'Thank you.' Propped in an armchair by the window with its border of stained glass sat a man crippled in every limb. Behind him the land outside the window dropped steeply. Industry stalked the greenery in the landscape; arthritis conquered the man.

'Dearest Michelle.'

'Ernst. It's so good to see you.'

'You should come more often.'

'I should. I feel pathetic that I give in to distance so easily. What seemed just around the corner now assumes travelling difficulties of mammoth proportions. How are you?'

'I keep trying these new tablets but they're no ruddy good.'

'Oh Ernst. I wish they'd find something to solve it.'

'They will one day. New breakthroughs in everything are coming thick and fast.'

'Change is everywhere. Is it going to be for the better?

I've been noticing a lot of things that puzzle me.' Michelle stopped talking when Ernst put a finger to his lips and nodded towards the door.

'Ask her for some coffee,' said Ernst almost inaudibly. Michelle picked up the vibes. She got up, stealthily making for the door, and opened it quickly. Sure enough the housekeeper was hovering in the hallway.

'May we have some coffee please?'

'*Ja*,' said the wooden face.

Ernst and Michelle sat quietly whilst they waited for refreshment. When it arrived, Ernst's undimmed blue eyes watched smilingly as Michelle took charge of the pouring. Small, bald, fair-skinned, with a still bushy moustache, he had gained a reputation as a man who gave meticulous attention to detail. Sadly there had only been enough family money to put his elder brother through law school. Ernst had had to make his own way. He had been in local government during the rebuilding period of Liga. How he'd fought for restoration, and how hard the battle.

'Not bugged, are we?' winked Michelle as she sipped the frothy coffee and helped herself to the spicy *Pfefferkuchen*.

'We can't get rid of the old habits,' chuckled Ernst. Then he became rather serious. 'I don't know where to start. I don't know whether to say anything at all. It may be no more than an old man's overactive imagination, but I'd never forgive myself if something happened and I hadn't warned you. A wall is something physical that you can see. If you want what is behind that wall, you break it down. This is something much more sinister. It has no wall.'

'Oh?' said a puzzled Michelle.

'Have you ever heard of a political party that has no

name, no recognizable form of dress, no manifesto, no headquarters and no official list of card-carrying members? That's why this is so difficult to explain. These people – and I'm more and more convinced they are not a figment of my imagination – are impossible, at the moment, to winkle out.'

Michelle pursed her lips in thought, took another sip of coffee, then asked, 'What facts have you?'

'None whatsoever. It's purely a gut feeling. This growth is feeding on unemployment. You know how irrational people are when they have just been made redundant. It's like a bereavement. You're willing to listen to anything that will give you a structure to cling to.'

Late morning came. The sun struggled out, melting the frost, which ran down the window.

'The same pattern recurs. A group of workers are made unemployed. Almost immediately there follows an act of violence targeted at an employed non-German. The attacker is rarely caught. When he or they are, they always belong to the group of recently unemployed. Now, Michelle, who is the catalyst that brings these two lots of people together?'

'Have you told the police?'

'It is suspected some of the police, doctors and local government officers belong to this nameless party. Why do you think the perpetrators of the violence are rarely caught? Why do you think so few crimes are reported? Often there are no bodies – who spirits them away? Member doctors treat their own members' wounds.'

Their coffee grew cold. Michelle shivered. 'I've had a feeling about that place all along. There's something fishy.'

'Where?'

'The nursing home where Ilse's mother is. Oh, they look after the old folk well enough, but too many things don't add up. What's a talented young doctor doing staying in the east, for a start? Why does he have an office in an old people's home when he's not the resident doctor? Why does he get called to cases of violence which are outside his area? Why does his mother dislike us sitting in the corridor? And . . . and . . . oh my God, Ernst, Mary's falling in love with the doctor.'

Ernst leaned forward. 'Michelle, get Mary back too England. Maybe the doctor's OK. Probably he's a young man who needs the extra money and doesn't know what he's getting into. I'm an old man, I can take the risk of being ridiculed or bumped off. Speaking out is one thing I can do for my home town. But Mary's young. There may be nothing in it. Things will sort themselves out, but while that process is going on, it's better she doesn't get in any deeper with the doctor.'

'Whew,' was all Michelle could manage.

'About the other two little matters. There's a backlog of about ten years, but my brother's been able to cut through the bureaucracy. Oh, and here's a photocopy of the plans from when I was on the council.'

Ernst handed her two manila-paper covered bundles.

'And now, lastly, a personal comment.'

Ernst was in full rhetorical flow by now.

'Go to England with Ilse. Stuff your silly pride and live on her money. How many people do you know who would go to the gates of a concentration camp to find you? Think how good she'll feel to be able to do something for you. She thinks she owes you. Everybody needs someone in their corner. The old lady's not got long, and Mary will have to make her own way. You need each other. You're good for each other.'

'Nobody's talked to me like that. I've always just seen my own angle, not wanted to put upon anyone.'

Michelle got to her feet with new vigour.

'I'll see you soon, Ernst. Take good care of yourself. And thank you. Thank you a million times over.' She kissed his forehead and held his misshapen shoulders.

When she looked back from the gate, the garden room was empty. The sun went behind the clouds and a chilly wind blew through the unkempt hedge, vibrating the dead and twisted creeper hard by the south wall. The house seemed to be unbearably lonely, craving someone to love it again.

31

On the sitting-room table was a note from Mary. She had gone out with her doctor friend. Ilse wasn't yet home. Since the full realization of her mother's condition had sunk in she had been brittle-tempered and difficult to live with. Darkness came early, and Michelle watched the city light up in shifts as people transferred from factories and offices to blocks of flats. She felt no ease of belonging.

'What on earth happened? I've told you about the streets at night,' shouted Michelle tersely as Ilse came in the door.

'Oh, not you as well,' returned Ilse, looking pointedly at the two empty sherry bottles on the coffee-table.

'I haven't drunk those,' said Michelle warningly. 'I'm having a clear-out.'

'Mutti was having a good day. She talked more. That's why I stayed on.'

'Good. I'm glad to hear it,' said Michelle.

Ilse unbuttoned her coat. 'We must talk soon about us going. Mary's got to get back to work and we've intruded on you enough. I can see you've a busy social life.'

'What do you mean? I haven't got a social life . . .'

'Well, you're always sneaking off somewhere, and when you come back you're so secretive. I'm sick to death of you "seeing a man about a dog".' Ilse flung her coat furiously onto the chair.

'Some things are better not talked about. It's for your own good.'

'And who are you to decide what's good for me?'

'Because I've had to live here and you haven't.'

Ilse was in the mood for emotional missiles.

'You don't talk to me any more. I feel like an acquaintance you've taken pity on because her mother's ill.'

Ilse flounced off down the hall, slamming the bathroom door after her and locking it.

Michelle followed, yelling at the closed door, 'And now I'm a cleaner and not a doctor, you pity me. I didn't talk because you've too much on your plate,' she screamed. 'I didn't talk because your home at Spatz Holz is a wreck. Ernst rents it. Factories blow smoke over it. Children and dogs pee in the garden. And I've got the deeds of the house for you. And the treasure trove might still be there. And I've got a map from Ernst showing where it is if Mary ever wants to do anything about it when she's older. I didn't talk because there's violence here. There's going to be a demo and you can bet your life it won't be peaceful. There are things going on here that neither of us ought to know about. I did it for you. I did it for Mary.' Gradually her battery ran down. She leaned against the wall, her heart beating rather fast.

The bathroom door opened. Ilse took her in her arms.

'Take me to England with you when you go home,' said Michelle weakly.

'You silly old bat,' said Ilse.

Michelle grew smaller, finally disappearing from view

217

when the railway track followed the curve of the river. Ilse was talking to herself; Mary couldn't make out the words. Her mother looked dreadful.

'She'll come, Mum.'

'Will she?' Ilse leaned against the head rest and closed her eyes. Later, the old medical case – Michelle always told Mary she could tell her age by the number of wrinkles in the bag – slid from the sleeping hand. Mary picked it up, reverently placing it on the seat next to her mother.

Mary finally added to her qualifications and started her own garden centre. She needed a partner, and who else would it be but Mike?

The memory of Dr Hoffman faded eventually. 'I don't know what I saw in him,' she said.

Ilse, threatened with blindness, was rushed to London, to have laser treatment for a detached retina. It was completely successful. Whilst in recovery, a young man came to sit by her bedside.

'Is there a particular record you would like me to play for you on the hospital radio?' he asked.

'I don't think so,' said Ilse, 'but thank you.' Then she thought again. 'I don't know if it's possible, but I like *The Blue Danube.*'

After much searching, the young man found the record in a London library. As the music flowed like the river itself, Ilse was young again. She and Mutti and Vati were sailing downstream on the brightly lit boat before the war.

A little while later the hospital radio tuned into the national news.

'It has been announced today that Berlin is to be the capital of a united Germany.' It added, 'A massive rebuilding programme has been launched to restore the industry and architecture of eastern Germany.'

Next day, with her unpatched eye, Ilse read the newspaper. It talked of British students spending their holiday time in Budapest and Prague teaching English, and of a new golden age in Europe. She laid the paper aside. Even a few paragraphs tired her. A new golden age in Europe? How, oh how, for Mary's and her contemporaries' sake she hoped this optimism would bear fruit. Maybe she and Michelle were wrong about what they saw in the future. Each year there were fewer of them – the generation who had lost their youth to political fanaticism. Too few to act as guides into a new Europe. Who would listen to the old?

'Please God don't let it happen again,' she said out loud. She felt the long shadows, the restlessness of the world's people on the move, and the beginnings of the second *Flucht*. Anxiously, she looked at the door for the one person she could talk to. A visitor came in with grapes and magazines.

'Hello, survivor,' said Michelle.

AFTERWORD

This book is dedicated to people of every race whose lives have been caught up in a whirlwind of war and politics but who have survived against overwhelming odds.

Many of us have been privileged to know people who lived through the tumultuous times during and after the Second World War. Sadly their number grows fewer. Many never told their full story; but years later, a sentence here, a memory there, snippets of conversation recalled, still reverberate. Mercifully for some the mind blotted out that which was too painful, whilst for others it was disturbing to talk at length about the past. They are men and women we see in the street carrying their groceries home; the man with the white cane and empty coat sleeve sitting on the park bench.

Some occurrences in the book did happen, but the characters and places are entirely fictitious.

Survival weaves together the fragments of several people's experiences to illustrate the fragility and strength of human endurance and sanity when powers beyond our control dictate our actions. Above all, it is a tribute to those who lost everything and survived to enjoy a return to more peaceful times, harbouring no bitterness against any race or country.